Serendipity

Serendipity

A Post World War II English Family Saga

THE FINAL BOOK IN THE 'SOMERVILLE TRILOGY'

MARY CHRISTIAN PAYNE

Sign up for the newsletter to get news, updates and new release info from Mary Christian Payne: http://bit.ly/MaryChristianPayne

Published by TCK Publishing
www.TCKPublishing.com

ISBN: 163161973X
ISBN 13: 9781631619731

Dedication

To JRP

May I have this dance?

Table of Contents

Chapter One

*I*t all began on a warm April day in New York City. Eugene Phillips had a plan. He thought it was a very good plan and could see no reason why it wouldn't work. All he had to do was get Kippy to agree to go along with it. And he could do that. He *knew* he could do that. He'd thought it all through carefully; thought of each and every obstacle in his path. It was ingenious and foolproof. Now the time had come to present the details to Kippy. Eugene had always been a good salesman. That's all it would take. Kippy trusted him. Always had. Edwina was gone, and so was Eugene's sister, Grace. There was really no one to stand in his way. No one who knew all of the details. As Eugene sat at a corner table sipping a gin and tonic, he spied Christian Crawford, a.k.a. Kippy, and waved a hand to him, as he crossed the upstairs room at the 21 Club in Manhattan. He was a few minutes late for their scheduled luncheon date and he moved rapidly toward the table where Eugene sat. Pulling out the chair opposite his uncle, he reached across and shook his hand.

"It's good to see you Uncle Gene. You're looking well. I'm glad we could get together while you're in the States."

"Thanks, Kippy. You're looking well, too. I can never get over how much you seem to grow each time I see you. How tall are you now? About six, two I'd guess?"

"A shade under that. I think I'm through growing. God, I should be. I'll be twenty-four before too long."

Kippy smiled and shook his head, and as he did so, memories of his sister, Edwina, came flooding back to Eugene. Her son looked remarkably like her. The same nearly turquoise eyes. The same thick hair, perhaps a bit darker, but still very blonde. He was actually better looking than his mother. He had a squared, masculine chin, an aquiline nose, and a firm mouth, with perfectly straight teeth. Eugene couldn't help but think of how proud Edwina would be of her only child. He thought of everything his nephew might have had, if Edwina had only lived. Or if she had done things differently. He *might* have been an Earl, and been addressed as Lord. Those thoughts brought a surge of anger, which had propelled him to meet Kippy on this day. It was time to have a long overdue conversation.

Eugene had not seen a lot of Kippy since his nephew's move to the United States. That was when Edwina had taken her son to their other sister, Grace Crawford's home, in Greenwich, Connecticut. The Countess had discovered that Edwina was involved, romantically with her husband, Nigel. It was then that she'd threatened to ruin Edwina forever. Obviously, the wisest thing to do at the time was to take Kippy and leave England. Kippy was just a baby. The year was 1941, and World War II was raging. Edwina's lover, Nigel Somerville, had taken care of all documents Edwina needed for passage to the U.S., as well as necessary funding. In Eugene's opinion, if the Earl hadn't been such a *Casper Milquetoast*, Kippy and Edwina would *not* have left England. Instead, the Earl would have divorced his wife, married Edwina, and Kippy wouldn't have grown up in the States.

At any rate, he *had* been taken from his homeland. He'd lived with his mother for a short time, while Edwina leased an apartment in Manhattan and began working for *Bonnie Cashin*, a well-known fashion designer. Kippy never returned to England. By the time Edwina might have wished for her son to be with her, she'd married Nigel Somerville following his wife's death. Unfortunately, they'd been married only a short time before her husband became very ill with Parkinson's disease, followed by a series of strokes. Shortly after, Edwina was stricken with cancer, which spread to multiple organs. During Edwina's last battle with that ghastly disease, Kippy was away boarding at *The Groton School*, in Groton, Massachusetts. He had been deemed too young to return for her funeral. Grace and Craig Crawford, Edwina's sister and brother-in-law, adopted him as soon as practical after Edwina's death, and Kippy became Christian Crawford, known to everyone as "Chris."

No one in his hometown of Greenwich ever called him Kippy. Nor did his classmates at Groton or fraternity brothers at Cornell. Gene was probably one of the few people who held to the old name, since that was the way he remembered his nephew. If things had worked the way they should have, Eugene firmly believed that his nephew would have become Lord Christian Somerville, but the Earl died before adopting him. There was considerable doubt about that possibility however, due to the Laws of Primogeniture, which forbid children not born biologically from inheriting titles. But, Eugene was stubborn, if not stupid, and he believed that if Kippy had only been adopted, the Courts would have found in his favor. It had been a rotten patch of luck all around. As a result, Kippy didn't inherit *Willow Grove Abbey,* the magnificent country estate owned by the Somerville family, and he didn't become a member of the gentry. Eugene knew that Edwina had wanted that for him more than she'd ever wanted anything. If that bloody Sophia Somerville Stanton hadn't intervened, everything would have been perfect. Sophia was the Earl's only daughter. Eugene's scheme would restore what was rightfully Kippy's, and prove to Sophia Stanton that she wasn't as smart as she thought she was. In addition, Eugene would profit too. He didn't intend to explain to Kippy how his uncle would benefit if Kippy were to find himself as the owner of *Willow Grove Abbey.* Not yet, anyway. The waiter came to the table and Kippy ordered a scotch and water. Then, he settled back and smiled at his uncle.

"What brings you to the States, Gene? I haven't seen you in what, three, maybe four, years?"

"Well, Kip, the fact is, *you* brought me to the States."

"I did? How's that? I'm always glad to see you, but do you mean you came specifically to see me?"

"Yes. I *do* have some other business to attend to while I'm here, but you and I are going to have a long overdue conversation. Grace and Craig never wanted me to mention the subject I'm about to bring up, but you're definitely old enough now to make your own decisions, and since they're both gone, I think it's time you knew the truth. Understand, I'm not being critical of my sister and her husband. I know they did what they thought was right for you, but I believe the time is correct for you to know the entire truth about your background. For you to decide what you want to do about it."

"I'm not at all certain I understand what you're talking about," Kippy answered. "Are you speaking about my life in England before I came to America?"

"Yes, but more than that. I'm speaking of what should have been rightfully yours. The Somerville family snatched it away from you. Snatched away what your stepfather, the Earl Somerville, and your mother, wanted you to have."

"Uncle Gene, I was a baby when Mother and I came to the States. I don't remember anything about the time I lived in England. I scarcely lived with my mother over there, as you know. Actually I scarcely lived with her over here. Most of the time, I was away at school. I never even met my stepfather. Of course, I remember my mother, but not vividly. It's almost as though my life began when I went to live with Aunt Grace and Uncle Craig. I always thought of them as my parents. Well, they *were* my parents, legally. They were wonderful to me."

Grace and Craig Crawford were killed in an air crash, traveling back to the States from Hawaii when Kippy was at Cornell. Since that time he'd felt he had no family. Of course, he had his mother's brothers and sisters in England. But, he'd never known them well. He was most familiar with Gene, and even that relationship was strained by distance. Kippy was still just a young man and craving the love of a family. He had loved his adoptive parents with all of his heart, perhaps even more than he had his mother. She was more a dream to him than a true memory. It was heartbreaking for him to find himself virtually alone. Thus, when his Uncle Gene announced that he was visiting New York solely to see him, Kippy was naturally touched and delighted.

"I know they were wonderful to you, Kippy. Moreover, I don't think they would be very happy at my bringing up the past. However, I think you need to know the entire truth."

"Is there something about my past that I don't know about? My parents were always honest with me. They always answered my questions about my mother, and my father, for that matter. At least, what they knew of him."

"It isn't a matter of honesty. I don't think they intentionally lied. There were just details omitted. The rest of the family thought it best if you didn't spend time dwelling upon things that couldn't be changed. I don't agree. I suppose I don't agree because I think that they may still be changed. But in order for that to happen, you need to know all of the facts."

"What are these 'facts' you're referring to?"

"How much do you know about your mother's marriage to the Earl Somerville?"

"Well, I know that he was somewhat older than she was. I know that he was the father of a friend of hers, and that he was a widower. Also that my biological father was a German Army officer and that the Earl Somerville helped my mother escape from Paris after she was trapped there, when Paris fell in World War II. I don't know exactly when they were married, or whatever happened to my real father. Anyway, my mother and the Earl married after the war. It was short-lived, because my stepfather became ill and died, and not long after that my mother also became ill. That's when Aunt Grace and Uncle Craig adopted me. When my mother died, they thought it best if I didn't return to England for the funeral. I was still very young, you know. I was at Groton at the time, and happy in school. I think they felt that there was no point in reminding me of matters that might cause me heartache.

"All right. Well, there are many other details, Kippy."

"Uncle Gene, please try to call me 'Chris.' 'Kippy' sounds completely foreign to me."

"All right, I'll try, Chris, but I can't promise I won't slip up. You've always been 'Kippy' to me. At any rate, I want you to understand that what I'm about to tell you may have an enormous influence upon what you decide to do with your future. So, please, listen carefully, and think about what I'm telling you."

Chris looked perplexed, and a bit anxious, as his uncle prepared him for the facts he was about to reveal. What in the world could possibly be so mysterious? Gene took off his eyeglasses and cleaned them with the napkin, examining each lens carefully, before putting them back on. Then, he motioned for the waiter and ordered another drink. Chris sat patiently waiting. After the waiter brought the drink, Eugene began to speak.

"Chris, if things had worked out the way your mother wanted, and for that matter, the way your stepfather wanted, you would not only be the owner of one of the most illustrious and renowned estates in all of Great Britain, but you would very likely have the title you were denied. Unfortunately, the Earl's daughter, Sophia Somerville Stanton, intervened and kept that from happening."

"Sophia Somerville Stanton? Who's she?"

"She and your mother were roommates at the *Ashwick Park School* in Kent. They were very, very close friends, practically sisters. They were inseparable. They pretty well grew up together, as they were just children when they met at school. When they graduated, your mother went to Paris to study fashion design and Sophia ended up marrying a Duke. However, she was a member of the landed gentry before she married the Duke. Her parents were the Earl and Countess Somerville and Sophia was Lady Somerville."

"I remember the name 'Somerville'.

"Nevertheless, Sophia's marriage to the Duke was very brief, and he died when she was pregnant. She inherited a great deal of money from that husband. He was rotten wealthy. She went to Paris for a get-a-way and ended up having her baby there. Your mother was the brick she leaned on. The baby was a girl. Her name is Isabella. That was in the fall of 1936. Sophia returned to England, and your mother stayed in Paris. Apparently, Edwina became involved with Sophia's father at some point. I don't know all of the details about that period in her life."

"Do you mean she had an affair with her best friend's father? God, Uncle Gene, that seems somewhat immoral, to say the least."

"She was still a young girl, Chris. Not yet twenty-two. I'm sure he swept her off her feet with his title and wealth. However, she did everything she could to resist because she felt terrible guilt over the betrayal of her friendship with Sophia. So much so, that she married your father, a German Officer, assigned to the French Embassy, who lived in the same building. I didn't know your father, and he was probably a decent enough fellow, but the times were wrong for such a union. The war broke out and he was called back to Berlin. Edwina refused to go, although she was pregnant with you. From my understanding, your father never even knew about you. It was shortly after that, when the Earl Somerville helped her to escape back to England. That was after Paris fell to the Germans in June, 1940."

"What ever became of my father? You mean my mother never even told him that she was pregnant?"

"She had to get out of Paris, and very quickly. She might have ended up in Germany, since she was married to a German Officer. She hadn't been pregnant very long when France was attacked. Of course I'm certain she intended for your father to know, but everything happened in such a rush. He had gone back to Berlin and Germans were marching down the Champs Elysees. Once she was safely back in Britain, it would have been very dangerous if he had known where she was. I don't really know what became of your father. I assume he was killed in the war. I don't think he ever knew about you, Chris. I'm certain he would have been thrilled to know that he had a son. I don't know if you have relatives in Germany. I suppose you do, although no one has ever looked into it, to my knowledge."

"So, what's the big mystery," Chris asked? "I mean, I knew most of this, except for the fine details."

"Well, to skip ahead. The Earl's wife, Countess Pamela Somerville, passed away after the war and shortly after that the Earl married your mother. Sophia Somerville Stanton was livid. They had already gone through an uproar over the affair. Sophia learned of your mother's involvement with her father and her wrath was over the top. Even though they had been the best and dearest of friends, when it came to the idea of Edwina becoming her stepmother, and worse still, inheriting money from her father, Sophia was adamant that she would do anything to stop that from happening. She caused untold problems for your mother and Nigel. Our family has always believed that Sophia's nasty behavior placed enormous stress on your mother and undoubtedly contributed to her illness."

"Was Sophia married? You said that her husband, the Duke, died?"

"Yes, she re-married in about 1940 during the war. That was probably part of the problem. Her husband is a physician, a psychiatrist, I believe. He's successful enough, but certainly not in the Somerville's class. Sophia had been used to having everything. And I do mean *everything*. *Willow*

Grove Abbey, the family home, is an incredible, magnificent mansion. Her husband could never come close to providing that sort of life for her. There's no question that Sophia assumed that when her father passed away, she would move back to *Willow Grove Abbey.* However, your mother almost brought that dream to a halt."

"What do you mean 'almost?'"

"Sophia insinuated herself into a situation in which she had no business interfering. Her father left *Willow Grove Abbey* to Edwina. Edwina, in turn, left the home to me, with instructions to hold it in Trust for you until you turned twenty-one. Sophia sued Edwina's estate, and because of her scurrilous threats and abominable accusations, I decided it was best to settle out of Court rather than have your mother's name dragged through the muck. We settled the suit out of court, at the last moment, when it became apparent that Sophia was intent upon making Edwina out to be a fortune hunter, a liar, a cheat, and, well, practically a whore. The Will reverted to the Earl's plans before his marriage to your mother. It was the Earl's *supposed* intention that the property was divided into thirds for his children. In effect, *you* were the rightful heir to *Willow Grove Abbey,* and the associated holdings, including *Somerville, Ltd.,* the family business, estimated to be worth some five million pounds. However, that was reversed by the Somerville family's law-suit. They won back the home and business. The Judge *did* make provisions for *you* in terms of inheritance."

"Yes, I know he did. I received a large inheritance from Nigel Somerville when I turned twenty-one. But in terms of the house, surely my parents fought for me?"

"No, Kippy...Sorry...Chris. I believe they felt that it was better to let things settle as they were. They simply wanted a new life for you. I'm certain they wanted no ties to Great Britain. They loved you very much and obviously wanted you to remain here in the States. If you'd known that you had an inheritance in England, they would've worried that you'd return there when you came of age. I thought perhaps that they *would* tell you the entire story when you turned twenty-one, but they didn't, and then they died, which was beastly. I feel you deserve to know."

"I *did* inherit a great deal of money from the Earl Somerville when I turned twenty-one. I remember that well. I had to sign a zillion papers and an investment account was set up for me. I remember that I received letters from each of the Somerville children and that they were all very gracious. They even told me that if I ever wanted to stay at *Willow Grove Abbey* to just get in touch with any of them and it would be perfectly fine. Apparently, the Earl had told them he wanted me treated well. That money made me very wealthy, Gene. I don't have anything to feel sorry for myself about. What difference does any of this make now? My mother is dead, the estate is settled, Sophia Somerville Stanton has her inheritance and I have mine. I can't change what went before."

"Ah, but perhaps you can, Chris. That's why I've decided to tell you all of this."

He stopped talking while the waiter served their food. Chris couldn't imagine what his Uncle meant. How could he possibly change any of the facts? When the waiter left the table, Chris resumed the conversation.

"What are you talking about, Uncle Gene? The law is the law. Yes, it would have been nice if I'd been the heir to a vast fortune in Britain, but apparently it didn't work out that way. I'm not exactly a pauper. Besides what Grace and Craig provided for me, Nigel Somerville was very, very generous. I really never understood that. I guess he did it for my mother. My adoptive father was quite well-to-do, you know. Now, I've graduated Cornell's School of Hotel Management and have an excellent position with Kaplan Hotels, International. I've a great apartment on the corner of Eighty Fifth Street and First Avenue, a large investment account, and I'm happy with my life."

"I know that, Chris. Moreover, I'm proud of what you've accomplished. But, I have some real anger about the fact that you were cheated out of what was rightfully yours. Your adoption by Nigel Somerville, and the accompanying title."

"Frankly, Uncle Gene, I think you're wrong about the title bit. It's my understanding that in order for a person to hold the title of Earl, he would have to be the eldest biologically born son of the deceased Earl. Even if I had been adopted by Earl Somerville, there's no way I could ever have held a title."

"Where did you become so knowledgeable about English titles?" Gene asked, frowning.

"When I was at Groton and my mother married into the nobility. A lot of the guys started ragging on me about being an aristocratic, titled Englishman someday. I didn't think for a minute that was true, but I got so sick of hearing it that I went to the school library and looked it all up. I read about the Laws of Primogeniture, which solidly say that the eldest biological son inherits. So, I know that I could never have held a title."

"Well, that's basically true. But, your mother outlived the Earl and he left her everything. *I mean everything*. She could do with it, as she liked. There is a Law that governs women's rights to do as they wish with their marital property. That means that she was able to leave it to anyone she wished and that's precisely what she did. As I told you, everything was left to you, and I was the Trustee."

"Are there no sons in the family?" Chris asked.

"Yes. There are two boys, older than Sophia. But, neither wishes to live at *Willow Grove Abbey*. One is married and has a magnificent estate in Scotland. The other is an Anglican vicar. Neither has any interest in the ancestral home. That leaves Sophia, her physician husband, and their daughter Isabella. It's probably true that by Law you could not hold the title of Earl. Then again, if Sophia's father had adopted you, who knows what might have happened? The Courts would have had to settle it and perhaps as the adopted son you would have had a precedent setting case. In any event, he didn't adopt you, so we shall never know."

"This is all ancient history, Gene. What do you want me to do about it now?"

"That all depends upon you. I'm simply here to give you facts. You can decide if you want to pursue it further. I mentioned Sophia's daughter, Isabella, earlier. Well, Isabella is now living in New York. She has graduated from the Rhode Island School of Design, and is a commercial designer. She works for Tate Motif's, which renovates old structures. Primarily old office buildings, hotels and so forth. You've probably heard of them."

"Yes, I have. They're a well-known, respected firm. In fact, our firm has contracted with them to renovate some of our hotels."

"Isabella is a beautiful girl. What I'm about to suggest won't be a hardship, I assure you. She'll not be in New York forever. Eventually she'll return to England. Her name is not Somerville. It's Stanton. She'll someday inherit all that was supposed to have been yours; *Willow Grove Abbey*, and a fortune. "

"And you're suggesting that I meet the lovely Isabella, woo her and win back my rightful inheritance by marrying her?"

"Ah, you catch on quickly, Kippy…Chris…My boy."

Chris looked down at the table and let the thoughts swirl through his mind. It was true that he had a good life. He had been educated well, and his prospects for the future were excellent. He didn't even know if he wanted to live in England. However, other considerations came into play as he sat there contemplating his Uncle Gene's outrageous suggestion. He was not afraid of hard work, had immersed himself in his new occupation and now, here was his Uncle, saying that if things had worked differently, he would not only be the owner of one of the grandest estates in England, he might even have had a title! He couldn't help but feel cheated out of what should have been his. He thought of his mother. It was those memories that caused the most consternation. He wondered if the reason his mother had married the Earl Somerville was because of the life it would have afforded her son. After all, the Earl was significantly older than she was and Chris believed his mother might have had anyone for whom she set her cap. What would his mother want Chris to do now?

"What makes you so certain that this Isabella would even be interested in me?" he asked Gene.

"Aw, come on, Chris. You have what it takes to sweep a young girl off her feet. Just look at you. You're better looking than any chap I know. Thank God, you haven't adopted this new way of running about with your hair down to your shoulders. Moreover, you're smart, refined, with a history of the best schools, and an excellent job. What young lady wouldn't be thrilled to have you?

"Well, one who's from the British aristocracy," Chris laughed, "and if she's as attractive as you've painted her, she may already be involved with someone."

"No, she isn't. I've done my homework. Yes, she's of the aristocracy, but she wasn't raised to be cheeky about such things. Her grandparents caused quite a kerfuffle when Sophia Somerville wanted to marry Isabella's father, Spencer Stanton. They felt that he didn't have the proper lineage, that he was not of their class. I gather both Sophia and Spencer vowed not to do the same to their daughter. Isabella lives in a modest flat in a brownstone on East End Avenue and appears to go about her life as any other working girl in New York. She has friends, of both sexes, but no special chap. She really *is* a knockout, Chris with masses of long, dark hair, and incredible blue eyes. A nice figure too. Why don't you just meet her and see what you think?"

"And how am I to go about that? I can't just phone her unexpectedly, and ask her to dinner."

"Surely you're smart enough to think of an innovative way to meet her. I can give you her address. It isn't far from your apartment. Perhaps you could arrange to run into her on the sidewalk."

Chris laughed. "I suppose where there's a will, there's a way. I don't know Gene; I'll have to think about all of this. The primary reason I'd consider it would be to avenge my mother. It sounds as if she was cheated royally."

"Oh, there isn't any question about that. Sophia Stanton went bonkers at the thought of having Edwina as her stepmother, let alone that she might inherit the family home and fortune. She was adamant that her father be stopped from making such arrangements."

"Why didn't my mother make certain that everything was ironclad?"

"She was very, very sick, Kippy. She hadn't the energy for a protracted legal battle. Before she'd time to really think it through, to grasp the fact that she was a widow and had a terminal illness, she herself died. I believe that the trauma she endured at the hands of Sophia hastened her death. She was terribly worried about you, which is why she sent you to the States. She would never have wanted you to be so far away from her at the end, if it hadn't been for her concern about what would happen after she was gone. If the Earl had adopted you, then you would have been a member of the Somerville family and would have inherited an enormous fortune and the family home, since the Earl initially left *Willow Grove Abbey* to Edwina. It was tragic."

Chris finished his salad and drained his cup of coffee. "Well, I appreciate your telling me these things, Uncle Gene and I'll mull them over. Where are you staying?"

"I'm at the St. Regis. Fifty-fifth Street and Fifth Avenue. Ring me after you've had a chance to think. I'll be here four more days, so perhaps we can have dinner one night."

"That sounds good. I'll check my calendar and be in touch," Chris answered, as he shook his uncle's hand. They began to walk out of the club together when Chris asked, "Why is this so important to you, Gene? I don't see that you get anything out of this."

"Not directly, no. However, Edwina was my sister and I'd like to see a wrong righted. I also wouldn't mind being related to the owner of *Willow Grove Abbey.*"

"Whew. You're way ahead of yourself. I haven't even decided if I want to meet this girl yet. Slow down, Uncle Gene."

Gene laughed to himself. If everything worked as planned, after Kippy married Isabella, he would be having the same sort of chat with Isabella, unless Kippy came through with a lot of money for his uncle to keep his mouth shut.

Chapter Two

When Chris left the Twenty-One Club, he walked down Fifth Avenue to the New York Public Library. There sat the enormous stone lions, which guarded the entrance to the massive structure, which stood between Forty-Second and Forty-Fourth, and fronted on Fifth Avenue. He showed his card and found his way to the area housing microfilmed newspapers of old. After quite a bit of searching, he found the *London Times*, dating from 1935 to 1965. He settled himself at a viewer and began to search the newspaper films. First, he came upon a studio portrait of Sophia Somerville, as a debutante in 1935. She looked breathtaking. It described her as one of the most sought after 'Belles' during that London Season. It also mentioned that she was Lady Sophia Somerville, daughter of the well-respected and esteemed Earl and Countess Somerville. In the very next day's *Times*, there was a large photo of an incredible mansion with a headline that said, *'Historical Willow Grove Abbey Site of Spectacular Debutante Ball.'*

It was a lengthy description of Sophia Somerville's "coming out" Ball, which apparently had been held at her ancestral home. There was another smaller photo of the magnificent ballroom, awash in flowers, and later in the evening a photo of the dance floor covered with exquisitely gowned ladies, and men in white tie. Chris continued to search through the films for more information about the Somerville family. He found many articles about Earl Somerville, and stopped to read them but they held little interest. The next clipping, which he found intriguing, was an announcement of the marriage of Sophia Somerville to Lord Owen Winnsborough, an enormously wealthy Duke. It described the wedding ceremony, held at the bride's home in an attached chapel named St. Mary and St. Edward. Chris was astounded that there were actually homes that had their own, private chapels. He took a break from the films and searched for information about the stately old homes of Britain. There he found a clear description of *Willow Grove Abbey*, and its history. He learned that it was one of the oldest estates in England and had been granted to a Somerville by Henry VIII when he ordered the dissolution of Catholic Monasteries. Chris was dumbfounded. He'd never imagined that the Somerville estate could be so ancient and so grand. He made a copy of the photos and the description, so that he could study them in more detail later. Then, he found the *Doomsday Book* and read more about the estate. Next, he found *Burke's Peerage*, which gave a marvelous genealogy of the Somerville family. He was becoming very, very intrigued. It wasn't so much that he believed Eugene's fantasy about Chris being able to become the Earl Somerville, but it was astonishing that his mother had once lived in that splendid, old manor house. Chris had always been fascinated by old structures. Nothing of such elegance was being built in the modern era.

He moved back to the microfilm, continuing his search of the *London Times*. From 1939 onward, the majority of the news was about the World War. He'd studied World History in college, and searched for books on that era, as it was clear that he didn't understand all that had happened during that period. He *did* come upon an obituary for Lord Owen Winnsborough, who had been married to Sophia Somerville and had died drowning in the Thames. There was a photo of him and Chris was surprised that someone as stunning as Sophia would have married such a mediocre guy. Perhaps it was simply a poor photograph, but he rather resembled a basset hound.

Before the day was over, Chris had come upon photos and stories about the well-known RAF Captain, Spencer Stanton, Sophia's second husband, who was knighted by the Queen for wonderful research he was doing at his own clinic. Apparently he was a psychiatrist. Sir Stanton was a marvelously good-looking man, quite an improvement over the first husband. There were many photos taken at his knighting ceremony and among them were several of his daughter Isabella. It only took one glance for Chris to see what his uncle had been raving about. The young lady was absolutely exquisite. He didn't remember ever seeing such a stupendously beautiful girl. Even in a news photo, which was not usually first rate quality, one could see her beauty. She greatly resembled her father, but there was a lot of her mother there too; the black, tumbling curls and bone structure. She looked to have a bow shaped mouth, with lovely lips, that made a fellow immediately think what it would be like kiss her.

After seeing her picture, nothing else really mattered. Eugene was certainly accurate when he'd said it wouldn't be a hardship to meet Isabella Stanton. Later in the films, he found a large color photo of her again, at her own debut. It was even lovelier than the other. Her dress was sensational and her black curls were piled on top of her head in an upsweep. In color, he could now see that her lips looked to be a natural, baby pink and her cheeks resembled the shade one found inside of a large seashell. The girl was divine.

He put everything back into its proper place and exited the library. It was over seventy degrees outside and the afternoon was fading. He decided not to return to his office for the rest of the day and instead headed for his apartment on Eighty-fifth Street and First Avenue, on the Upper East Side, one of the most posh neighborhoods in the city. Ever since Chris' graduation from Cornell University, with his MBA in Hotel Management, he had loved New York City. Of course he'd lived there three years when a small boy, after leaving England. But now he knew the city intimately, and had many, many friends, both from Groton and Cornell, as well as a group he was close with at Kaplan International. He walked East over to Lexington Avenue, turned North and continued until he arrived at Bloomingdale's Department Store at Fifty-ninth and Lexington. He debated whether to jump on the IRT Line, which would carry him by subway up to Eighty-first Street, but decided it was such a glorious spring day that he would continue to walk. He passed flower stalls on practically every corner, selling armloads of daffodils and tulips. The trees that lined the avenues were coming into bloom, and he slipped off his suit jacket, as well as his tie. Tucking the tie into his suit pocket, he slung the jacket over his shoulder. He felt young, successful, and happy.

While Eugene's impromptu meeting had concerned him, after having learned more about Isabella and her family, he was now more interested in meeting her. He really wasn't much interested in the story Eugene had painted for him, but he was definitely intrigued by the characters he'd described. Chris was not at all certain that he really had any desire to leave New York. However, it certainly might be marvelous to live in that ages old mansion. Still, he seemed a bit young to bury himself in the English Countryside. In addition, he had absolutely no interest in settling down with a wife yet. The only plausible reason that might have made him consider Eugene's rather spiteful plan was the fact that his mother had wanted him to have everything that accompanied the Somerville lifestyle. It angered him to think that because of foolish jealousy on the part of Sophia Somerville, his mother's final wishes for him had not come to fruition. Of course none of this was Isabella Stanton's fault. He had no ill will towards her. There was simply a strong desire to right what he saw as a dreadful wrong. Obviously, Chris didn't have the *full* details about everything that had taken place. Perhaps if he had, he might have felt differently.

When he arrived at his apartment on the corner of Eighty-fifth Street and First Avenue, he said hello to the doorman, stopped to pick up his mail and caught the elevator before it ascended. Chris had the Penthouse apartment in the eleven-story building and every friend he had was green-eyed with envy at his catch. It was a rent-stabilized building, which meant that when he signed the lease, the rent could go up no more than a small percentage, no matter how sky-high prices rose in the future. Rent could not be raised until Kippy moved out, or until his salary reached $200,000 a year. It was nowhere near that now. He planned to stay in the City until either his rent or salary rose significantly, or until he married and had children. That wasn't on the horizon for a long time to come. His long-term plans were to raise a family in Greenwich, which was undoubtedly one of the wealthiest suburbs in the United States, so he knew that he had his work cut out for him. But, he was a hard worker, extremely intelligent and very good-looking. And he already had a comfortable nest egg, thanks to the Earl Somerville and Craig Crawford, his adoptive father. In a day and age when the term 'hippie' was being used for the first time, Chris was an employer's dream.

The apartment was on the top floor and upon entry, one stepped into a large, sunken living room, rectangular in shape. The floors were polished hardwood and a lovely old oriental rug covered them, with lots of reds, hunter green and beige. Straight ahead from the entrance door was a wall of glass, part windows and part French doors providing entrance to the penthouse garden rooftop. At each end of the large living room, there were short hallways, each leading to a private bedroom and bath. Behind the wall at one end of the living room was a bigger than ordinary kitchen, by New York standards. In addition, there was a small powder room off the living room. Chris had furnished it in a lovely style, especially for a bachelor. When his adoptive parents had died, he inherited all of the furnishings in their Greenwich home. Of course his apartment was not nearly large enough to accommodate everything from a large home, so he had stored the majority and selected only those pieces that he wanted to move to Manhattan. Thus, the décor was certainly eclectic. In the living room there was a lovey, black leather sofa, with large matching ottomans. Behind the couch was a sofa table, where sat numerous photos of his family, in silver frames. In front of the couch, there was a large, square cocktail table of teak wood. Magazines were scattered across the top, from *Architectural Digest*, to *Town and County* and *GQ*. On the wall opposite the couch was a quite large television, with bookcases built on either side. There were two other chairs in the living room, both of calf's leather. In one corner sat a black Steinway Baby Grand piano. There was a small bridge table and chair set, which was perfect for dining alone or as a couple. At the other end of the living room was a dining area, where sat a magnificent, antique Queen Anne dining set, which seated six people. Both bedrooms were fit with lovely bedroom suites, in modern design and both were covered with Merimeko fabric spreads.

Chris made himself comfortable on the leather sofa in the living room. He pulled the paper he had copied at the library, with the article about Isabella's debut, from his suit coat. There was no question that she was a beauty and he would be lying if he said he didn't want to meet her. He went back and forth throughout the evening, contemplating whether to become an accomplice to Eugene's scheme, or to let it be. He would never have considered it, if Isabella had not been such a knock-out. He did not rest easily that night and was tired at work the next morning.

He put the whole idea out of his head and concentrated upon what needed to be done at the office. He had an eleven o'clock meeting with commercial realtors who were interested in selling an eight story building on Manhattan's East side, near East End Avenue and Sutton Place. His company had been thinking for some time about buying a building in just such a location, and turning it into a boutique hotel. It would be small by New York standards, but very elegant, so it definitely needed the proper upscale address to match its planned upscale prices. The major problem Kaplan International had was the difficulty there might be obtaining the necessary permits for such a project in that area. There was sure to be a ruckus from some of the neighboring brownstones, and other buildings in the neighborhood. The building was on the Registry of Historical Buildings, so certain guidelines would have to be strictly adhered to. It was quite near Sutton Place, one of New York's most exclusive and prestigious neighborhoods.

After his meeting with the realtors, Chris decided to attend a cocktail-dinner being held by Mayor John Lindsey at lovely Gracie Mansion, the mayoral home, that evening. The dinner was specifically designated to be an informal way for those interested in the sale of the building. People could meet and discuss logistics. Chris had not been going to attend. He really loathed that rather phony sort of evening, with everyone trying to get the Mayor's attention, in order to ask favors. But, the perceived project was definitely going to call for a good relationship with the Mayor, so he knew it was best to attend. Such things were part of his business, and he did what he needed to do. Later in the day, he also telephoned his Uncle Gene at the St. Regis Hotel and told him he was tied up with business that evening, so they made plans to dine the next night at L'Aiglon, which was right across from the St. Regis. After lunch Chris grabbed a taxi and went over to have a look at the building they were considering making an offer on. He exited the taxi on Sutton Place and walked over to East End Avenue. There sat the building his company was quite interested in. It was well kept, and attractive, constructed from red brick, with black shutters at the windows. It already had the look of a small hotel. He peered inside, and saw that the flooring in the lobby was an attractive black and white marble. There was certainly room for a front desk, and lounges for guests to relax in. All in all, from what he was able to ascertain, the spot looked ideal for what Kaplan International had in mind. For its age, the structure looked to be in very good shape. He had an appointment to see the entire building on the next day and was looking forward to it. The next step would be to negotiate a price, and to make decisions about renovations. If they were to get the bid, and actually go forward with renovating the building, it would be a massive project. There'd been nothing like this done in New York for a long time. It would be Chris's first attempt at such an important project and it was very important to him that it be done correctly.

Chapter Three

April 16, 1964

That evening, Chris presented himself at the entrance to Gracie Mansion for dinner with the Mayor. That magnificent house, built in 1799, was located in Carl Schurz Park at East End Avenue and 88th Street. It was a short distance from Chris's apartment. The old colonial home was stunning. There was already a group of people lined up for entrance to the enormous main floor rooms. The crowd entered very quickly and everything was in perfect order. Mayor John Lindsey stood in a receiving line to welcome his guests. He was a debonair, athletic, buoyant man; very handsome and virile. You could see that many of the women present were hoping to do more than simply shake his hand. As Chris was waiting his turn, he noticed that right in front of him was a stunning girl. Doing a double take, he was certain that it was Isabella Stanton! Of course, she was much older than the pictures he had viewed at the New York Library, when she would have been just out of her teens. Now she appeared to be in her mid-twenties. But there was no doubt that it was Isabella. She had that same shining, black hair, shorter now, but still falling to her shoulders. She had brushed it back from her forehead, and brought both sides around to the back, where they met and were secured by a lovely ornamental clip. Chris had never seen skin such as hers in his life. Her cheeks were baby pink and so smooth they resembled fine porcelain. He wanted to run his fingers across them, as he knew they would feel like velvet. She wore small pearl earrings in her ears, and a pearl cross at her neckline. She was dressed in a very attractive ensemble. It was a navy twill blazer suit, double-buttoned in brass at the waist, and the blazer rode down over a short, flared skirt. Its blouse was ribbed white cotton, with a high, small collar and long sleeves, with cuffs that shot out below the sleeves of the blazer. She looked elegant with just the right amount of panache. He *had* to meet her.

Once through the receiving line, he accepted a glass of champagne from one of the white-coated waiters circling the room with trays. Then, he strolled about the magnificent room, never letting his eyes stray too far from Isabella. She seemed very comfortable in her surroundings. He noticed her chatting to several different people, both male and female, but she did not seem to be attached to any one person. After about a half hour, the guests were led into a grand dining room where an enormous table was beautifully set with lovely china, silver and crystal. There were place cards at each seat. Chris found his, and stood behind the chair. Glancing over to his right, he looked down at the place card next to his. He was filled with delight, when he saw the name *Isabella Stanton* written clearly upon it. What a lucky thing to have happened. He might have spent months trying to find a way to meet her, and here she was, seated next to him at a dinner. Soon, she appeared at his side and he welcomed her and introduced himself. She, in turn, said that she was Isabella Stanton and that she was happy to meet him. It was obvious that she was schooled in social graces, and not the least uncomfortable in such a setting. She spoke with a pronounced British accent, which added to her charm. Her hands were long and slender and she had lovely nails. Everything about her shouted 'class'. He held her chair for her, as everyone took their places and they settled in, placing their napkins on their laps.

"You obviously have an English background," Chris said, as he looked to his right, into her remarkable blue eyes. "Either that or a Commonwealth country," he added.

"Yes. I'm always called on it immediately," she laughed. "I'm British. I grew up in a country area, near a small town called *Bedminster with Hartcliffe*. But, I've also spent a good amount of time in London, and also in *Tunbridge Wells*, where my parents lived after the war. I came over here to attend the Rhode Island School of Design and then took a job at Tate Motif's. Have you been to England?"

"Well yes and no. I lived there as a small child. My mother was English. I was actually born in Paris, but the war came along shortly after I was born. She was in Paris working as a fashion designer. When Paris fell, she returned. Then, in 1941, she brought me to the States. She had a sister living here. My mother went back to England after the war, and I was supposed to join her, but was away at Groton, so stayed through the semester. Then, Mother got cancer and passed away, so I never went back. I was adopted by my aunt and uncle here."

"What a sad story. But, you've had a good life, then, with your adoptive parents?"

"*I had* a good life with them. Wonderful. They lived in Greenwich. It was a terrific place to grow up. But, while I was at college they were killed in an air crash on their way home from Hawai'i."

"That's simply dreadful. You've had more than your share. So, what then? Did you come to New York after college?"

"Yes, I have a degree from Cornell's School of Hotel Management. I was hired by Kaplan Hotels International, for their development division."

"How interesting. As I said, I'm with Tate Motif's, and my specialty is renovation of old hotels."

"Is that what brings you here tonight," Chris asked.

"Yes. Probably the same as you. This talk about the building on East End Avenue, near Sutton Place, is interesting. What do you know of it?"

"Our company is bidding on it. I think we have an excellent chance to get the job. This is *my* project. It would be restored and made into a boutique hotel, very upscale. I suspect a fight with neighbors. Then, there are all of the permits necessary. You know what that means. Union negotiations. The works. I'm glad Mayor Lindsey planned this evening. Hopefully, it will start the ball rolling."

"Yes. I see quite a few well-known people in the hospitality arena. I also see a number of the old silk-stocking group who have been living in and running the Sutton Park neighborhood for generations. They will be hard nuts to crack."

"Are you personally acquainted with any of that set?"

"Yes, actually. One lady. Lady Childers-Long is an acquaintance of my parents. She has a home in England as well as the townhouse on Sutton Place. She's really a charming person, one of the 'old guard'. She was very kind to me when I first moved to America. Sort-of kept an eye on me, you know. I wouldn't say that I'm close with her, but close enough that if I had to ring her and discuss this new hotel, I wouldn't be uncomfortable."

"That's good information to have. It could well come in handy. I assume that you're putting in a bid to do the renovations for the hotel?"

"Yes. Tate Motif's is the best, in my opinion. We're painstakingly accurate when it comes to authenticity. We take extraordinary time to get details correct. If your company gets the bid, I hope you'll consider us. Here, let me give you my card." Isabella reached into her small handbag, which rested on the table, and produced a crème colored business card, with her name, and company engraved upon it, along with her office address and telephone number. *Damn, no home number*, thought Chris.

"Here, let me give you mine too. Have you been to see the building? It's really very nice."

"Only the exterior. I'd love to see the interior, but don't want to put carts before horses. I'd rather wait to see if we get the bid. And I cannot make a bid, without seeing the interior."

"I'm going to see the interior tomorrow with a realtor. If you'd like to join us, I'd be happy to arrange that."

"Oh, how lovely. And how nice of you. Yes, I'd love to. What time?"

"I don't know with certainty. If you'll be in the office in the morning, I'll give you a ring."

"Yes. I shall be. Perfect. I'll look forward to your call."

Well, it's only a business appointment, but I'll see her again tomorrow. Maybe we'll have lunch, Chris thought.

The dinner progressed smoothly and he thoroughly enjoyed his conversation with Isabella. Not only was she engaging and beautiful, but she was also obviously intelligent and personable. If he hadn't already known that she came from a wealthy, titled family, he would never have guessed it. She was very down-to-earth. He truly did want to know her better.

The following afternoon, he picked her up at her office, on Madison Avenue and together they traveled by taxi to East End Avenue. There, they exited the cab, and walked the short distance to the building under consideration. The realtor was waiting for them in front. Chris introduced Isabella to her. Her name was Mrs. Carter and the three of them entered the building. It had once been a private home, in the early 1900's, then an office building, followed by a co-op apartment. Now, it stood vacant, awaiting its next reincarnation. They took the elevator up to the first floor and walked down the long hallways, stopping along the way to explore what had once been office suites or apartments. The interior was in excellent condition. Of course, it would need a complete facelift, in order to make it into a deluxe hotel facility, but it was in amazingly fine shape for its age. The rooms were large and there were numerous bathrooms. It was evident that the best design would be one that did not create a 'cookie cutter' hotel, with all of the rooms the same, but instead one with different contours for each accommodation. Chris and Isabella talked as they strolled through the property.

"I think it's utterly charming," Isabella said, as they peeked into various nooks and crannies. "It could be transformed into a very special and unique Inn."

"Yes. I agree. What would you think about naming each room or suite, after an English village or landmark? Since England is your homeland that would be particularly suited to your skills. Plus, you know that Americans are kooky about anything British."

Isabella laughed. "I love that idea. Of course, that would mean that the décor would also be of an English character, some in a formal, period look, and some in a more cottage-like atmosphere. The more luxurious suites could be named for English Kings and Queens. Those of a cottage nature could follow in the footsteps, perhaps, of English authors, or characters from classics—'Jane Eyre', 'Charles Dickens', 'Anne Hathaway', and of course 'Shakespeare'. Also, there are the Romance poets, 'Elizabeth Barrett Browning', and so forth."

"Great concept, Isabella. I can almost picture the design of the various rooms. We will have to come up with a name that fits the English theme as well. That shouldn't be difficult. England is filled with charm."

"So, you've decided definitely to make a bid on the property?"

"Yes. Definitely. I think it's perfect for the purpose we have in mind. Have you decided definitely to bid for the design contract, if Kaplan International gets the building?"

"I'd need to discuss it with my superiors, but I would just love to dig my heels into such a project. This is the sort of thing I dream about."

"Well, I wish I could just tell you that I would definitely award you the contract if our bid is successful, but it has to be done on a fair basis. Others will be invited to offer their designs and quote their prices, as well."

"Of course," answered Isabella. "I understand the business. I'll have to put pen to paper and look at the numbers. In addition, before I get anywhere near that stage, there is going to be the working out of an agreement with the neighborhood association, unions and so forth."

"Yes. And you have an advantage there, since you know someone in the neighborhood. I can relate that to my superiors."

Mrs. Carter was not a hard-sell sort of person. She let them walk through at their leisure and occasionally pointed out some element or another that needed to be highlighted. She also explained about the property taxes, which were astronomical, but Chris had expected that. They would be taken into account when room prices were set. Kaplan International worked with an excellent accounting firm, and the CPA's who were employed to worry about such problems.

When they finished their inspection, Chris and Isabella thanked Mrs. Carter and Chris told her that he would be in touch with her no later than the next afternoon. As far as he knew, there were not a lot of others bidding on the site. He looked at his watch. It was twenty minutes after eleven, so he turned to Isabella and suggested that they grab a bite to eat before returning to their respective offices. She readily agreed. Hailing a taxi, Chris told the driver to take them to the Plaza Hotel, where he planned on dining with her in the Edwardian Room or The Oak Bar, whichever Isabella preferred.

Chapter Four

"The Edwardian Room, for lunch!" Isabella exclaimed. "Oh no, Chris. I'm sorry, but I keep those sorts of places for special occasions only. The Oak Bar will be fine. I just hate to be rushed in such exquisite surroundings as the Edwardian Room. If you agree, shall we save it for another time?"

They were in a taxi, driving south, toward the Plaza Hotel. "Yes. That's fine. I wanted to go wherever you preferred. I agree, actually, The Oak Bar would be better for lunch." Chris was very pleased to hear Isabella say that she wanted to save the Edwardian Room for another time. That meant she must assume that they would be seeing one another again in a social venue. They left their taxi in front of the palatial Plaza Hotel at Fifty-ninth Street and Fifth Avenue. It had such history, and elegance and was one of Chris's favorites. Isabella too, loved its historic charm. They walked up the wide stairs to the entrance and then onward to the back, where the Oak Room was located. Luckily, there was an empty booth in a quiet corner. They both settled themselves comfortably, and a waiter brought them menus. Chris would have considered a glass of wine, but wasn't certain that Isabella would, so he held off. He didn't want her to think he was a three-martini lunch person. She ordered a Cobb salad, and he ordered a French dip sandwich.

"So, if we're fortunate, this could end up being a really terrific opportunity," Chris commented, regarding the hotel project.

"Yes, I'm very keen on the idea. I'm anxious to go back to my office and start looking at a budget that would cover the ideas we've discussed.

Frankly, I don't think the décor would be beastly expensive. The St. Regis, for instance, is decorated in magnificent, French antiques from the Louis XVI period, which had to have cost the designer's a fortune. They are all authentic. What I have in mind for this hotel would be more in the category of 'shabby chic'. Not too 'shabby', but not too 'chic', except for the Period suites." She laughed. "One thing you haven't mentioned is whether or not there would be a restaurant?"

"Yes, most definitely," Chris replied. "It would really be a necessity, I think. There are no grand restaurants over in that area, and room service would naturally be expected in such an upscale property. So that décor would also have to be figured into the cost analysis."

"Very upscale, or again, shabby chic, or would there be two, one for breakfast and luncheon, and another more formal, for evening dining?"

"I think perhaps two. Maybe one in the style of the English cottage look we discussed and then for evening dining, a really quite elegant atmosphere, what people imagine Buckingham Palace to resemble."

"You just smashed my budget to smithereens. Buckingham Palace? Chris, it really *has* been a long time since you were in England."

"No…No, I'm not that much a fool. I know it couldn't be anywhere near as incredible, but I'm just imagining a ballroom sort of interior."

"I'm joshing. I think I know what you have in mind. Perhaps gold leaf and tromp l'oeil treatment. Gold leaf chairs. Draperies from ceiling to floor, in puddles."

Yes. Exactly. I really do hope you come up with the right figures Isabella. You have a wonderful design concept, I can tell already."

"I'm going to put my heart and soul into it, but I really don't expect any preferential treatment. I think you'll find that you don't need to give me favorable reviews."

Chris was impressed with her self-confidence. She wasn't a braggart. She just appeared to know what the depth of her talent was. He was anxious to see her presentation. "Of course, I don't have the property for Kaplan yet, so I shouldn't get ahead of myself."

"When does the bidding begin?"

"I intend to call Mrs. Carter and place an offer this afternoon. There is only a week in which the present owner will accept offers, so I hope we're lucky. Isabella, do you think you would be able to do me an enormous favor? Please, don't feel that I'm taking advantage of our very new friendship, but I think your contact with Mrs. Childers-Long, whom you said you know from family acquaintance, might be an incredible help. Would you mind if I phoned and asked her to lunch, using your name as an introduction? I'd like to woo her with our tentative plans and assure her that the property would not affect the neighborhood in any negative way."

"Absolutely. I'd be happy to. In fact, I'll go you one better. I'll phone her myself, and invite her to tea. Then, while I'm discussing the property, I'll mention your name and tell her that you will undoubtedly be ringing her."

"Perfect! I appreciate that a lot."

The waiter brought their luncheon orders and they stopped talking, and silently ate for a few moments.

"Do you get back to England often?" Chris asked in between bites.

"Not very. Once a year for certain. Perhaps twice. I try to go at the Holidays, always, and then again in the summer months. Summer is my favorite time in England. Our house is so gorgeous then. It's hard to describe my attachment to it."

"Tell me about it."

"Oh. It's so enchanting. Chris, it was built before Henry the Eighth's time. It sits in a grove of willows, birch, beech and ash trees, and has a chapel attached to it, with an ancient burying ground, where my ancestors have been laid to rest for generations. I think I may have told you that it's named *Willow Grove Abbey*. It truly was an Abbey once, until Henry VIII caused all of the monasteries and so forth to be closed, when England ceased to be a Catholic nation. The house was then granted to a Somerville ancestor. There has always been a Somerville in residence since that time, except for a very brief period when my grandfather re-married. After he died, the new Countess inherited. She died and left it to *her* brother, if you can imagine. We had to go to Court to win back our estate, but we did. It is palatial, Chris. 22 Bedrooms, most with their own baths. A captivating ballroom. Lovely drawing room, grand dining room. On and on."

"Who will inherit after your parents are gone?"

"I'm not really certain. My uncle, Blake inherited, as he is the eldest son, but he and his wife live in Scotland, at *her* ancestral estate. My other uncle, Drew, is an Anglican vicar. He lives in a small village, with his wife and children. So, when we won the lawsuit the family brought against Grandpapa's second wife, my parents bought out the two thirds that my uncles owned. Things have changed so dramatically since the war. It's becoming just about impossible for the landed gentry to keep up the old estates. Many have had to sell off priceless art works and even open their homes to the public for a fee. We're fortunate, as my father does very well with the clinic he owns. But, I suspect with taxes what they are, eventually we shall be faced with the same sort of dilemma. So, to answer your question, I don't really know. Now that my parent's own it outright, I suspect that I'll inherit.

"Do you think that you'll return to live in England some day?" Chris asked.

"Probably. I love New York, but I've never given up my citizenship, and I'm a Brit, through and through. I cannot imagine staying here forever. Hopefully, I'll gain enough experience and then eventually return to England and perhaps open my own design studio in London."

"You're family home sounds unbelievable. Like what you read in historical fiction. I'd love to see it."

"Perhaps someday you will," Isabella smiled, as she finished her salad and took a last drink of tea.

They ended their lunch and left the Plaza. It was another splendid, spring afternoon, and Chris wished they could lazily stroll up Fifth Avenue, back to their offices, but he needed to contact Mrs. Carter and he also knew that Isabella was anxious to start on a budget. So, he hailed two taxis and they went their separate ways. Before the cab sped off, Isabella promised him that she would call Mrs. Childers-Long and invite her to tea as soon as she reached her office.

Isabella kept her promise, and with great good fortune, Mrs. Childers's Long was available for tea on the following afternoon. They made plans to meet at the Waldorf-Astoria at half after two. Isabella arrived and entered through the Park Avenue lobby; a cavernous space, decorated in the grandeur of 1931 Art Deco. Of course it had been updated, but the 1930's had been amazingly preserved. As luck would have it, she was led to a table right next to the Cole Porter piano. Cole Porter was a resident at the Hotel from 1939 until only recently and he had often played that very piano. Isabella sat down at the lovely, round table and surveyed the scene. She was perched above the main lobby and had a vantage point to witness the coming and going of visitors and guests. So, while she watched for Mrs. Childers-Long, she enjoyed the hustle and bustle of New York passing in front of her. It was only a few moments before she spotted her acquaintance and stood to make certain that she was seen. Mrs. Childers-Long gave her a small wave and made her way to the table. She was an attractive, older woman, with striking platinum hair, worn in an elegant upsweep. She had on a lovely silk summer dress, with long sleeves and a squared neckline. It was classic and probably designed by someone renowned. Isabella had been having a bit of difficulty of late trying to choose clothing she liked. The styles had definitely changed enormously, the lengths of skirts and most dresses were what people called "Mod." Isabella's taste ran toward classic, so while she had brought the hemlines up a bit on her skirts and dresses, she hadn't bought anything very trendy. She admired her friend's lovely day dress.

"Mrs. Childers-Long. How lovely to see you. It's been so long. I'm so happy you could join me for tea on such short notice," Isabella exclaimed.

"Please dear, call me Sarah. I feel ancient enough, as it is. Let me feel as though I'm your friend and not your Granny."

"All right, Sarah, but I don't think anyone would ever take you for my Granny," Isabella laughed. "You're looking splendid. I was just admiring your dress. It's lovely."

"Thank you, Isabella. I bought it at *Bergdorf's*. If you want to find clothing that still looks ladylike, that's the place to go."

"I'm glad to hear that. I've had a hard time lately. Everything is so very short. I'm not tall anyway, and I just don't feel right in these miniskirts."

"You're a classic English girl, Isabella. You can't beat the English for putting out a perfectly charming lady, still."

"Thank you, Sarah. So, how have you been? Have you been here all summer, or are you leaving soon?"

"Yes, leaving soon. I came over after the Holidays, and am ready now to spend a beautiful summer in my Country home in Somerset. I hope to see your parents while I'm home."

"They would love that. They're both working very hard, but are wonderfully happy. My father's clinic is doing so well. Did you know that he was knighted?"

"Yes, I did know that. So wonderful. I know you must be very proud of him. I can just see your mother's exquisite face now, beaming with love and pride."

"Yes, that is spot on," Isabella replied. "I went over for the ceremony. It was very moving."

"What are you doing now, my dearest? I haven't seen you since you left design school. Obviously, you're working in the city."

"Yes. I'm a designer with Tate Motif's. It's quite well known for its wonderful renovations of historical buildings. That's my specialty."

"How divine. That must be very rewarding; to see something old and beautiful restored to its intended plan."

"It is. In fact, that's one of the reasons I hoped to be able to speak with you, besides simply wanting to see you and catch up on happenings. My company may be involved in a project in your neighborhood."

"In my neighborhood? Well, it *is* an old area. Where precisely are you speaking of?"

"The very old building on East End Avenue, not too far from Sutton Place. Not terribly large. Red brick. Do you know which I mean?"

"Yes…yes. It's vacant, I believe. It's still well-kept but nobody in the vicinity likes to have an empty building on the block. What is the plan for it?"

"A small hotel. What we call a boutique hotel."

"Oh dear me. I can't imagine a hotel in our neighborhood. All of the strangers coming and going. Traffic worsened. Taxi cabs all over everywhere."

"This would be a very upscale establishment, Sarah. The company that is hoping to buy it is Kaplan International, whom I am certain you've heard of. They have very fine, five star properties. This hotel would be small, and cozy. Have you ever been to *Number Sixteen* in London?"

"I've never stayed there, but I know its top drawer. Is that the concept for the building in our neighborhood?"

"Similar, only more posh. If Kaplan gets the contract, I'm hoping to do the design work. I've a wonderful plan, based on English style. There would be lots of chintz's and canopy beds, vintage tea sets on all of the tea tables in each room; Spode, Wedgewood, Havilland, and so forth. The grander rooms would have vintage sterling. Mahogany encased tubs in the baths. I'm sure you can envision what I'm describing. And you needn't worry about taxis going to and fro. We have spoken of having a Rolls Royce to meet passengers at the airport, take them to their meetings, dinner engagements, shopping…whatever."

"That sounds perfectly lovely. Perhaps, that sort of establishment wouldn't be an eyesore or a detriment. Of course, the Historical Register Organization would have to see it that way. But, you know, I'm on the Board, so I just might be able to be of help to you."

"That's what I was hoping, Sarah. The fellow from Kaplan, whom I'm hoping to work with on this project, is in total agreement with my concept, so I could assure you that it would be done properly."

"And, what is that chap's name?"

"Chris. Christian Crawford."

"Christian Crawford. But, of course I've heard of him. He's gaining a fine reputation for doing very good work. I don't know very much about him, but I know I have heard the name. Do you know much about him, dear?"

"No. Not really. I know his mother was English, and she had Chris during the war, in Paris, when she was married to her first husband. She came to America when Paris fell, and didn't go back until much later. Chris was really raised here. He went to Groton and then *Cornell*. When his mum died, he was adopted by his aunt and uncle and grew up in Greenwich. I guess she re-married back in England."

"Yes, she certainly did. And you don't know to whom?"

"No. I don't believe Chris and I have ever discussed it."

"Well, my dear, she was your step-grandmother! She married the Earl…your grandfather, Nigel Somerville. I believe he died and then so did she shortly thereafter. She was nearly thirty years younger than your grandfather. She left *Willow Grove* to Chris! I can't believe you didn't know this."

"I'm dumbfounded. I don't believe Chris knows that there is a connection between his family and mine. Surely he would have told me. So, it was Chris's biological family that we sued in order to win back our ancestral home?"

"Yes, dear. I don't know all of the details, but the general consensus among the gentry was that Edwina married your grandfather for his fortune."

"Oh Lord! Chris is nothing like that. He's a very hard worker and has already made a success of himself at a young age."

"Well, perhaps the fact that he was raised apart from his mother had an impact. I don't know, Isabella. I'm not certain whether you should say any of this to him. I have no desire to harm him or his reputation. Let me ask. Are you involved with him in a way that goes beyond business interests?"

"No. Well, I find him very attractive. We've only been to a formal dinner at the Mayor's mansion where I met him, and then had lunch yesterday. But, we get on very well. I should like to see more of him."

"Well, then sooner or later you will have to discuss this with him. My word of advice would be to wait and see if the relationship progresses. If so, see if he mentions it. If not, you will have to, don't you think?"

"Yes. Certainly. Of course, I don't want to hurt him either. I'll have to tread lightly, if he doesn't know any of this."

"You're a wise, intelligent girl, Isabella, just like your mother and father. See where your friendship goes."

Sarah and Isabella enjoyed a sumptuous tea and chatted about other things, but Isabella did not forget what she had been told. It worried her greatly. *Was there animosity between his family and hers?*

At the end of their lovely tea, Sarah Childers-Long made an exceedingly nice offer to Isabella. "My dear, since you are bound to have to persuade a bunch of old bats of the wisdom in allowing a hotel to be a part of their neighborhood, perhaps I can be of some assistance. Before I leave for England, would you like me to set up a get-together for people on the Board and other interested parties to come and hear your ideas and to vent any arguments they might have against it?"

"Sarah. A bunch of old bats?" Isabella smiled.

"Well, perhaps I shouldn't refer to them as such. I suppose I'm one too, although I don't like to think it. It would have to be soon, probably on the Tuesday next."

"I think it's very, very generous of you to offer to do such a thing. I know Chris would love to do that. It would give him the jump on anyone else. But, I'm pretty certain he'll say 'wait to see if our bid is accepted."

"I would think that sounds wise," Sarah responded. "When does he think he'll know?"

"In one week. He's putting in the bid to the real estate company today. So, he'll have a week to wait. In the meantime, I'm madly putting together figures, in the hope that I can land the contract to do the design work."

"All right. Then, ring me as soon as you know and if it all turns your way, I'll invite a group to my townhouse and you can take it from there."

"You are a true treasure. I hope you don't think I rang you just because I hoped for your help in this? I'm so happy to have seen you. I do hope we're able to keep in more frequent touch, either way. Even if I end up not involved in this project, I really would love to see more of you."

"We will just make it happen, won't we? I've so enjoyed our outing. Mostly seeing you and how you have blossomed. Of course, you always were the prettiest thing."

"Oh Sarah. I hope I can look like *you* when I'm your age."

Sarah patted Isabella's hand. "Darling girl. You'll always be a lovely creature. I so admire you young people, with the whole world at your fingertips and no ghastly war on the horizon to muck up your youth."

"We *are* fortunate in that respect. Of course, this Vietnam thing is creating quite a stir. I hope it doesn't escalate into something greater."

"Oh dear, I certainly hope not. You would think the world would have had enough of war. Nothing is ever accomplished, except ruin and heartache. Thank goodness, England seems to be keeping out of this."

"Yes, I'm very glad," Isabella answered. She took out a credit card and paid the bill and the two ladies weaved their way through the tables, and to the main entrance. They embraced and gave kisses on each other's cheeks. "Lovely to see you. Do call when you have more news. Thank you so much for tea. It was scrumptious." With that, Sarah Childers-Long hopped into a taxi, like a spy youngster and rode on to whatever her next appointment was.

Isabella decided to walk a bit. She was still knocked for six to have learned that Chris Crawford was related to her. She tried to remember if she had ever mentioned her mother's maiden name to him. She didn't think so. It seemed very unlikely that he had the slightest notion there was a family connection. She decided not to mention it right away. Sarah was right. If their friendship grew into anything more serious, then surely it would just naturally be discussed, in the course of learning to know one another better. There was no question that she thought that he was a wonderful chap.

Chapter Five

April 18, 1962

E ugene and Chris sat at the third table on the right. L'Aiglon was a beautiful restaurant, decorated lavishly in period French, with an overabundance of red velvet. It might have been taken for a French bordello, but the food was much too good for that. Gene ordered the mushroom soup, along with the mushroom caps stuffed with minced veal, and the veal chop L'Aiglon, a sautéed veal chop on a bed of green noodles with baked melted cheese on top. Chris ordered Pate Maison, Cold Vichyssoise, and Lobster in Shell L'Aiglon. They had Zabaglione for dessert, which was prepared tableside. Naturally, this all called for an excellent French Chardonnay. While they sipped their wine, they talked.

"So, Chris, tell me everything that's happened since I last saw you. Have you given more thought to my suggestions about Isabella Starton?"

"So much has happened that it's hard to know where to begin. Believe it or not, I met her, completely by accident. I've been assigned a new project that has to do with the renovation of a building near Sutton Place and I attended a dinner at Gracie Mansion that the Mayor held, for all parties interested in the project. My company wants to buy the building and transform it into a boutique hotel. Isabella works for Tate Motif's, a design firm that restores old buildings to their original state. She was at the dinner too. Seated next to me, no less. My God, she is an absolute knockout."

"I told you," Eugene replied, wiping the corner of his mouth with a napkin. "Did I exaggerate?"

"Not a bit. She really is something." Kippy took a sip of his wine.

"So, *now*, how do you feel about my idea of getting you back into *Willow Grove Abbey*?"

"Frankly, Uncle Gene, I think you're insane! I don't intend to try to play any games with Isabella. She is the type of girl a guy dreams about. I'd be an idiot to mess this up by lying."

"You needn't lie. Just don't let her know everything that *you* know. After all, you wouldn't have known these things if I hadn't told you. What if you'd met her yesterday and we'd not had lunch the day before?"

"I don't feel right about that, Gene. It's fortunate enough that I've met her without any planning or subterfuge on my part. Let me just see where this thing goes. Plus, I have a lot on my plate right now. This new project I'm hoping to take on will be keeping me very busy. What I really hope is that Isabella will be doing the interior design for the project. That way, I'd be able to get to know her much better."

"Does she seem to like you?"

"Oh, who knows? I think so. At least as friends. She is very comfortable in her own skin. God, she has to know she's gorgeous. She's probably heard it a million times. But, yeah. We get along pretty darned well."

"When will you see her again?"

"I'll call her in a day or two. I don't want to scare her off by seeming too anxious. I'll probably ask her to dinner. Or the theater. Or both." Chris laughed.

"Well, I'll be leaving on the morning flight to London, so you'll have to keep me informed by letter. Don't forget to do that."

"I won't, Uncle Gene. But, honestly, your dumb idea, about me marrying her for her wealth and the house are just not going to fly. My biggest problem now is whether to tell her that I *am aware* that we're sort of related, by marriage. It wouldn't worry me, except, that if there had been a real problem between my mother and Isabella's family, I might not be very welcome. She may even have very angry feelings about my mother. So, I think I'm better off to just let it go for the time being and let her get to know me better before I spring that information. But, she could also be angry about my not having mentioned it when I first met her. Jeez, See, I'm already in a mess."

"You *did* know that her mother's maiden name was Somerville?"

"Well, yes. I remember those papers I signed about the Trust, if nothing else. I knew that she'd married Earl Somerville, but she always referred to him as either Nigel, or the Earl. Anyway, I don't think Isabella has even mentioned that his name was Somerville. Maybe she did, but I don't remember it. I was too busy staring at her." He smiled again and blushed.

"Well. Chris. Even if my initial intentions turned out not to hit pay dirt, I'm pleased that you find Isabella enchanting. Even if it isn't your intention, you may *still* carry through on your mother's plans for you."

If I do, it will be purely by accident. I have no intention of taking part in any scheme like you've described. Anyway, I find it pretty hard to believe her parents are so awful, when she is very close with them and they've done one incredible job of raising her."

"Sorry, Chris. I don't know a whit about her father, but I can tell you that I sat in a courtroom with Sophia, Isabella's mother and she is a royal bitch! Don't tell me she isn't a bad person! She said some of the most vile, unbelievably rotten things about your mother. I wouldn't even repeat them to you and mind you, this was in front of numerous others. That's why I stopped the lawsuit. People in London would love to have gotten hold of such garbage."

"Gene, I'm really not the least bit interested in Isabella's mother. But, I'm *very* interested in the daughter. She's just a very, very nice girl, besides being gorgeous; a rare, one of a kind girl."

"Perhaps she has her father's disposition. I've heard he's quite remarkable. Did she tell you he's a knight?"

"No. I know he's a well-known psychiatrist and that he operates a clinic in the Midlands. I gather he's also an author. Supposedly he's quite renowned."

"Quite. You might say that. Queen Elizabeth knighted him for the work he's undertaken in rehabilitation of military chaps who suffered terrible mental anguish due to the war. The clinic has established a worldwide . It's grown to include others who suffer from traumas of various sorts: war, of course, both men and women, and various other sorts of abuse. Rape victims, brutal crimes and the like. I believe they've recently opened a new wing for addictions. There's been a terrible increase in that area."

"Yes, I'm seeing some of that here in New York City. The Vietnam conflict is causing a lot of it, from what I hear. Drugs are easy to come by in Eastern Asia."

"Could that conflict affect you, Chris? You're of an age to be drafted by the U. S. Army, aren't you?"

"Yes, but they haven't implemented a full draft scheme yet. Anyway, I'm not a U.S. citizen. I've always held on to my British Citizenship. My adopted mother, Grace, kept hers. I don't know why, really. Just some sentimental attachment, I suppose. Many times I've considered applying for citizenship, but I never have. Now, I'm glad I didn't. I don't want any part of this war. Don't misunderstand. I love America, and will forever think the Yanks were really special the way they stepped in and saved England during World War II. If this were a war like that one, I'd be first in line to enlist. But, it isn't. I don't know your views, but I don't think we've any business over there."

"Well, Chris, England isn't involved and I hope it stays that way. We still have a long way to go before we fully recover from what the Germans did to us."

"I never asked you, Gene, but did you serve in World War II?"

Gene blushed furiously. "No. No Chris. I was…well, I was judged unfit. Flatfeet, you know?" He laughed half-heartedly. "Also, beastly vision. I'm afraid I wasn't considered military material."

"But, then you must have been placed into a job connected with the war effort?"

"Yes…well…I wrote training manuals for new recruits. I suppose my book store experience made me top pick for such work."

"Yes, well, I was certain you must have had something to do with the war effort."

"Nothing terribly heroic, I'm afraid."

Chris changed the subject. "Do you know whether Isabella's father served? Wait…I think I remember reading that he was a POW. Really awful."

"Yes, Sir Spencer Stanton was quite a renowned RAF pilot. A Group Captain. Shot down over France, and spent four years in a German POW camp."

"God, no wonder he decided to devote his life's work to war victims." I'd like to meet him someday. I'll bet he could tell some stories."

"Well, Chris. I guess this is 'farewell' for a spell. Do write to me, even if you think my romantic scheme is a bit over the top." It probably *is*, but aren't you glad it led you to learn more about Isabella? Who knows where this might lead?"

"Oh. I'll never be sorry about that part. But, I've always believed that if something is meant to be, it will happen anyway. That's what seems to have happened in this case. They were just finishing up a last cup of coffee, laced with brandy. "Are you a believer in religion, Gene? I've never asked."

"I have my own beliefs. My Dad was a non-believer – an Atheist. But, he didn't push it off on us. Mum was a devout Christian Scientist. I think most organized religion is so much poppycock. I suppose if I had to name my beliefs, they would be a throwback to the Theosophists of old. They were all the rage, you know. At any rate, I'm not aligned with any main-stream church. What about you, Chris?" He took another sip of his coffee.

"I was raised quite strictly Anglican. But, to be honest, I know more about the rituals than I do the dogma. I'm interested in History of Religion and someday I'd like to take a course on the Bible and its historical signifi-cance. I can't really say what I believe."

"Well, get ready to think about it. Isabella's mother, Sophia, converted to Catholicism when she married Spencer Stanton. Isabella was raised in a solidly Catholic household. No birth control Chris. No sex before mar-riage. That will be a bit of a hardship on you," he chuckled.

"No, actually, she wouldn't find any argument from me. If that's her strong belief, I'm sort of impressed. I haven't met an honest to God virgin since I was sixteen!" He burst out laughing. "It's a nice thought that she doesn't sleep around. I think over half of the eligible girls in Manhattan do. I guess I shouldn't complain, because it makes it all very simple. But, you know, there's something very neat and tidy about a girl who is old-fashioned enough to save herself for marriage. I like that idea."

"You have a good head on your shoulders, Chris. I'd say some girl is going to be very fortunate, indeed."

When Chris arrived back at his apartment, after dinner with his Uncle Gene, the message light was blinking on his answering machine. Chris pushed the 'play' button 'to retrieve the message. "Hi Chris. This is Isabella Stanton. I had tea with Lady Childers-Long. It was a success. She wants to have a little 'do' at her townhouse for her neighbors and the members of the Preservation Board, in two weeks, on a Saturday afternoon, to help with your quest! I'm thrilled and thought you would be too. Now, you *have* to get the bid." The machine clicked off. He rewound it, and played it again, not because he hadn't heard it correctly the first time, but because he loved hearing her British accent. He immediately telephoned her back, and thanked her over and over for the part she had played in getting Sarah Childers-Long interested in the hotel project. They only spoke for a few moments. She told him that she had to rush, since she was going away for the weekend. He wanted to ask where she was going, and more importantly, with whom, but didn't want to seem inappropriately curious. After all, it was really none of his business. He didn't want to act like a lovesick boy. She had to know the power that her beauty had over anybody, especially a guy three years her junior. That bothered him. He'd never dated anyone older, although three years wasn't that much. *Still, he wondered if she might think him too young for her.*

When an entire week had elapsed, he received a call from Mrs. Carter, at the Real Estate Company representing the owner of the building under consideration for the hotel project. It was good news. Kaplan had won the bid! *Now,* he had cause to phone Isabella. His heart was soaring as he dialed her office number. *Oh, please let her be in…Please….Please.*

"This is Isabella Stanton. May I help you?"

"Isabella, it's Chris Crawford. Kaplan got the bid! I just found out."

"Oh Chris, that's simply smashing. Now, may I send my bid over to you?…or is it too soon?"

"No. No. I'll phone the other two firms that are interested and ask them to submit figures by the end of the week. I'll also call Sarah Childers-Long and tell her to go ahead with her plans for the afternoon get-together at her townhouse on Saturday."

"Perfect. So, today is Monday and the meeting will be Saturday afternoon. When will you make the design decision?"

"On Friday. Even if by some strange happening you don't get the contract, I'd definitely be grateful if you would come to the meeting with me and introduce me."

"I'd be happy to Chris and I *do* believe I'll get the contract. I know exactly what you want in the look and feel of the hotel and I've given you a huge price break. My profit won't be very much, but the high profile nature of this project would make it very valuable for Tate Motif's."

"Get your figures to me. I suspect that you're right. I haven't even met the other two designers. You're way ahead of the game in that we already agree on the over-all theme."

I'm putting them into an envelope now, and will be sending them by messenger. They should be at your office within the hour. Call me on Friday, when you've made a decision."

"I'll do that, Isabella. I'll speak with you Friday then. Goodbye."

"Goodbye, Chris."

Chris sat still, with the telephone receiver in his hand, while all that could be heard was a dial tone. The memory of her voice was in his head. He absolutely adored her British accent. She sounded so well-bred. So lady-like.

Chapter Six

May 2, 1964

*I*sabella got the contract for the hotel project. Hands down. Her ideas were superb, which Chris had already known and the cost estimates were far below what his budget called for. Chris was ecstatic. He immediately telephoned and told her the happy news. She sounded completely thrilled.

"Would you like to have dinner with me and celebrate," he asked.

"Oh, splendid. I'd love it, Chris. Where shall we go?"

"Are you kidding? This is the reason we saved the Edwardian Room. Remember, you said a 'special celebration.' Let me make a reservation for eight o'clock tonight. I'll pick you up at your apartment and we can take a taxi from there. Let me make certain I have your correct address. I know you're quite close to me."

"600 East End Avenue. The lower level. I'll be ready about 7:30. Taxi's may be difficult to come by."

"I'll get one on my corner, and then swing by to pick up you. I'm looking forward to it. See you then, Isabella."

Chris was never nervous when he took a girl out on a date. He wasn't the nervous type. But, this wasn't just another girl. And it wasn't just another date. This was Isabella and it was their first, real date. Not a business luncheon. Not a meeting to look at an old, empty building. This was the Edwardian Room, and The Plaza Hotel, with one of the loveliest girls in all of New

York City. It was a night to remember and of *course* he was nervous. He was one step short of shaking when the taxi arrived in front of her building on East End Avenue. He told the driver to wait while he jumped from the car and walked down the few steps to her doorway. He took a deep breath and raised the door-knocker. One rap and it immediately opened. There she was. She wore a pale lavender taffeta skirt that just reached her ankles. that had a wide band at her waist, which looked to be about 18 inches around. The skirt fell into lovely, feminine folds. The organdy blouse was white, ong-sleeved with a Victorian collar trimmed in lace. The front was pin-tucked and there were embroidered flowers scattered across the bodice, in pink, lavender and green. Her long hair was swept up with the curls softly arranged on top. She looked like a girl from another era. A 1910 portrait brought to life. Chris was speechless. Isabella's porcelain skin looked fresh and glowing and she wore very little make-up. Perhaps a bit of pink blush on her cheekbones and a light slick of gloss on her already naturally pink lips. *How could he possibly have found this magnificent creature?* He felt something he had never experienced before and he was intensely aware that her nearness was having an effect upon him. It was hard to choose his words.

"Isabella, has anyone ever told you that you look as though you just stepped out of a turn-of-the century portrait?"

"No. But I like the concept," she smiled. "Thank you."

"I mean it. You are absolutely breathtaking. Radiant. I'm…. I'm… blown away."

"Gosh, Chris. You look pretty smashing yourself. I love double-breasted suits on men who can wear them. You definitely are one of those."

He wore a midnight blue, double-breasted, worsted suit, with a crisp, white shirt, and a Regimental rep tie in stripes of dark blue and red. His streaked blonde hair was combed to the side. He wore a Cornell class ring on his right hand. Together they made a striking couple. As they walked into the Plaza Hotel, passers-by glanced twice at them, admiring their handsome looks, and trying to figure out who they were. They presented a refreshing change from the scruffy hordes of young people one saw loitering around midtown, and especially Greenwich Village.

The Edwardian Room was so exquisite that both Kippy and Isabella were highly impressed. If she looked like she had just stepped out of a turn-of–the-century portrait, their surroundings matched perfectly. There were magnificent chandeliers sparkling above them and the tables were all covered in pale pink cloths. Each was round and accommodated four persons. Kippy ordered a bottle of Rombauer Chardonnay, and they split a plate of Calamari. Kippy had Sea Scallops and Isabella had Shrimp Scampi. At first they talked more about the hotel project, but then the subject changed to more personal areas.

"Isabella, tell me more about yourself. I know about your growing up years and your home, but exactly when did you come over to America? Did you go straight from school in England to school in the States?"

"No, after my debut, which isn't even done in England anymore, my parents took me on a wonderful Mediterranean cruise. It began in Istanbul and then we sailed through the Greek Isles, Italy, Capri, the Italian Riviera, and the French Riviera and on to Barcelona. I learned so much. It's a trip I'll never forget. I fell in love for the first time on that cruise. At least I thought I'd fallen in love." She laughed, and took a sip of wine.

"Ah ha! Who was the lucky guy?"

"An Italian, of course."

"Oh…that makes sense. Every girl has to have her one Italian romance, doesn't she?"

"I guess so. His name was Lucca. He was really something else. I fully intended to come to America for one year of school, and study Italian at the same time, with plans to return to Italy and marry him. When we left to come home, I wept and wept, telling my parents that my life had ended. They were very wise. They didn't act like I was stupid, but told me to give it a year, and then see how I felt. Of course, it was all over by then."

"Did you keep in touch with him?"

"Oh yes. He even came over here to Rhode Island to visit me when I was in school there."

"So, he really was serious?"

"About as serious as any Italian man ever gets. I still write him occasionally, but the romance died out long ago. I wouldn't be surprised if Lucca isn't married by now. Of course, that wouldn't keep him from seeing me, if I showed up in Venice." She was laughing again.

"Poor guy. He may be still pining away for you."

"Somehow, I don't see Lucca pining away for anyone. It's more a matter of 'loving the one you're with'."

"Well, I'm glad you changed your plans. I'd hate to think we might never have met."

"Yes. That would be frightfully sad," she smiled.

It was just going to be a goodnight kiss. Something that had become an expected gesture at the end of any evening out with a girl. But, again, this was different. It began with their lips softly touching. She put her lovely, slender hands against his chest, and he encircled her in his arms. But, it didn't stop there. The kiss grew more intense and her arms encircled his neck, while he tightened his hold, to draw her closer. Both of their lips parted slightly. She reached up and placed a hand on the back of his head and ran her fingers through his hair as the kiss went on. Finally, they broke apart, both gasping for breath. She stepped away from him and they both simply stood there, drinking each other in with their eyes.

"Isabella. I'm overwhelmed. What can I say? I've kissed dozens of girls, probably hundreds, but none of them was anything like you."

Pearls gleamed at her throat. Her eyes moved steadily up, looking seriously into his. "We've known each other three weeks Chris."

"And oh. About six hours," he laughed, checking his watch.

"So, this is all nonsense," she murmured.

"You don't really think that." He followed the direction of her eyes, as she glanced about herself, looking a bit lost. He said quietly, "Three weeks is an age. I *knew* you after the first three minutes."

She smiled. "And I saw you staring at me in the queue at Gracie Mansion. But, Chris, I promise you, you don't know me. Not really. It isn't quite as simple as you think. Honestly."

"I'm too young for you. That's the one snag I can see. If that's what you're…'

"Of course it isn't, but…"

"But, nothing then."

"Three weeks and you don't know…"

"Whatever it is, I've plenty of time to find out. I suppose there's some guy…some man.

"No, there isn't."

"In that case, Isabella. My beautiful Isabella."

"The wine has gone *straight* to your head!"

"Listen, if you don't think I'm too young and there's no grand love affair in the background, you might as well accept the fact that whatever happens now, I won't let you go."

"Chris, you *must* slow down. We have so much to learn about one another."

"What do I need to learn?" he asked earnestly.

"I don't know with certainty. Perhaps it's me who needs to learn. If I ask you into my flat for an after dinner Port or Brandy, will you give me your word that we'll *only* talk?"

"I promise," Chris smiled and made the sign of the cross. Isabella unlocked her door and turned on several more lights. Chris followed her and settled himself in a chintz loveseat facing the small fireplace. She poured them each some Port and seated herself across from him in a small club chair.

"So," Chris began. "Before we go any further, let me say that you have a very pretty apartment."

"Thank you. My mother and I found it when I moved here. I like it."

"Now. What is it we need to discuss, Isabella?"

"When I had tea last week with Sarah Childers-Long, she spoke of you."

"Me? I've never heard of her, or met her, in my life. How does she know me?"

"She doesn't. She *knew of* you. More specifically, she *knew* of your mother."

"My mother? What did she say about my mother?"

"Chris, I'm a bit reluctant to share our conversation. I don't want to upset you. I don't know what you do and don't know."

"Excuse me, Isabella, but I haven't the foggiest notion what you're talking about."

"Well. I guess there's nothing for it but to come right out and ask you. Did you know that your mother was married to my grandfather, the Earl, Nigel Somerville?"

Oh Shit, thought Chris. Where do I go from here? I really care about her. If she finds out I knew who she was when I met her for the first time, she's likely to be really angry and also suspicious. I think I'd better act like I didn't know.

"Your grandfather and my mother? Are you kidding me? What are the odds of *that* happening? What was your grandfather's name?"

"I just told you. Lord Nigel Somerville. Your mother married him and became Countess Somerville. In effect, she was my step grandmother."

"I knew she was married to an Earl. Honestly Isabella, I never knew the surname. I may have heard my mother refer to the name Nigel."

"Chris, are you being totally honest?"

"Yes, of course. Why wouldn't I be?"

"Because there was a lot of hard feeling between our families. Specifically your mother and my mother."

"Why? Because my mother married your grandfather?"

"Well. He was in his seventies. Um. They had been involved in a long-term affair while my Gram was still alive, plus your mother and my mother were boarding school roommates."

Is there any way that she could ever find out that I inherited a lot of money from the Earl Somerville when I turned twenty-one? If so, she'd know with certainty that I'd heard the name Somerville before. She would be aware that I'd known about the connection between us when I met her. Damn. I wish I'd told her the minute I met her at Gracie Mansion. Damn Gene. I wish he'd kept his mouth shut. Now it's too late.

"This is all crazy, Isabella. I can't believe that we're actually sort of related through a marriage. How often would something like this happen?"

"My father always says he doesn't believe in coincidences. He would call our sort of meeting "serendipitous." He believes things are meant to happen."

"I believe that too," Chris replied. "So, all right. We're sort of related. That's great, I guess. Whatever happened between your mother and mine shouldn't be any concern to us."

"No. I don't suppose. Still, I'm not going to say anything to my parents about my having met Edwina's son. Mummy and Papa are very sensible and I don't believe it would influence their feelings about you, but I would rather wait."

"That's cool." Chris threw his arms into the air. "Hey! I'm an openbook. Whatever works for you is fine with me."

"Chris, while we're having an honest chat, I want you to know my feelings about pre-marital sex. Perhaps I'm putting the cart before the horse, but I'd rather get it straight right at the beginning. The fact is, I don't do it. Don't believe in it."

"I respect that. I'd never do anything you didn't want. I'm glad you feel that way and I'm glad you told me. I'd never try to convince you to act or feel any differently."

"That's important to me. If what you're looking for is…well, in England we'd say a *'quick shag,'* I'm the wrong girl. I made a promise to myself a long time ago."

Chris laughed heartily. "No, I'd never take you for a *'quick shag'* sort of girl. Don't worry. I can be celibate too."

"I'm well aware that most girls these days are just the opposite. Most everyone I know sleeps around. But, I never have and I'm not going to start now."

"I find your attitude refreshing, to tell you the truth. It makes you even more special to me."

They continued talking until nearly four o'clock in the morning. Chris was even more intrigued than he had been when the conversation started. Isabella's eyes were closing and she looked very sleepy. He wisely stood up and brought the night to an end.

"I'll see you tomorrow at Sarah Childers-Long's gathering. Would you like me to pick you up? It's supposed to be a gorgeous day. We can walk if you like."

"Yes, I'd like that a lot. Thanks for taking the time to talk, Chris. I sometimes have problems with trust, when I meet fellows. I don't know why. I suppose it's because I'm pretty quiet about my background and I'm suspicious that someone would be interested in me for my family money. I've been burned a couple of times because of that. So, I've learned to keep my mouth shut, at least until I know someone better, or if I think the friendship might become something more serious."

"Well, hey, that makes me feel great. I guess if you decided to talk to me about all of this, you must think that our relationship might be going someplace."

She laughed. "I suppose that's true," she nodded. "But, don't let it go to your head."

"You've already gone to my head. Sorry," he responded, as he took her into his arms, and kissed her again, with much more ease. He would have liked to kiss her all night long. But, he now understood the rules and he had no intention of breaking them.

He loosened his arms and she kept her head resting on his shoulder. "I really do care for you, Chris. Thank you for being so understanding. I'll look forward to tomorrow."

"I'll be here about 12:30. Until then," he answered, and gave her one quick kiss.

She closed the door and he began to walk the short distance to his apartment. The sky was the unique grey that comes along before the pinks and reds of sunrise appear. The remnants of a white moon hung in the sky. Isabella filled his thoughts. Everything seemed so perfect, yet he was frightened that something might go awry. He wished that he had never lied to her about anything, and once again cursed his Uncle Gene for even suggesting an unscrupulous scheme concerning Isabella. He kept wondering if he should tell her the truth right now, at the beginning, before they became any further involved. But, if he did, even at this early stage, it would be very clear that he'd been willing to consider the stupid scheme. He would not reveal it to her and would hope that she never found out.

Chapter Seven

DECEMBER, 1964

*H*e liked Mrs. Childers–Long immediately. She was a typical upper-class lady, and the addition of an English accent gave her even more élan. Plus, she clearly had a sense of humor.

"Well, don't you two make a splendid couple?" she remarked as Chris and Isabella entered the foyer of her lovely townhouse on Sutton Place. You're quite a posh young man, you know. If I were younger, I'd give you a run for your money, Isabella."

"*Sarah*!" Isabella laughed. "I thought there was a dear gentleman across the Pond. What would he think?"

"Oh my dear, at his age he'd probably congratulate me on my good fortune." She gave a hearty laugh and patted Chris on the back. "Come. Come. Meet my neighbors," she said, as she waved her arm about the parlor, pointing out her guests. It was an elegant room, decorated in period French, with delicate pastels of pale pink and green in both upholstery and window treatments. The décor "fit" Sarah. A maid appeared in a traditional European black uniform, with a white apron and cap. She bore a tray laden with a variety of hors d'oeuvres. There was coffee and tea on the table in front of the sofa. Chris helped himself to coffee and poured Isabella a cup of tea. Then, Sarah clapped her hands together and asked for everyone's attention.

"Dear friends. This young, handsome man is Christian Crawford, who represents Kaplan Hotels International, and this dear, young lady is Isabella Stanton, whom I must tell you I know from my very own homeland. Her mother and father are dear friends of mine. Isabella is a designer with the firm Tate Motif's. Both Christian and Isabella are very enthused about a project their companies have taken on. They're here to speak with you about it and to answer any of your concerns. Christian, why don't you begin?"

Chris stepped forward, into the center of the room. Sarah had arranged chairs in a circle, so that all present could see and hear him. Every chair was occupied. The crowd was comprised of mostly older people. At least in their sixties. And Chris could guess from the expressions on their faces that most were not one hundred percent in favor of the hotel concept.

"Good afternoon, ladies and gentlemen. As Sarah said, I'm Christian. Chris Crawford. I represent Kaplan Hotels International, which I'm sure most of you are familiar with. We're about to undertake an exciting project in this neighborhood, with your approval, of course. Now, when most people hear the word 'hotel', the picture that comes to mind is of a thirty story tall, rectangle, all glass and chrome. Well, that isn't at all the concept we have in mind. This would be known as a Boutique Hotel; Small, very upscale, very exclusive. It's a terrific location. How many of you are familiar with the old, empty building on the corner of East End and Sutton Place?"

The majority of those present raised their hands and nodded. "Well, with luck and hard work, in a little over a year, that eyesore will be reincarnated into the most desirable place discriminating visitors to New York can stay. It will afford the opportunity for the ultimate in luxury, as well as a calm, quiet haven for those who wish to stay away from the typical tourist crush of Manhattan. We anticipate that a lot of our guests will be from other countries. Thus, they will probably have had some exposure to this style of hotel. They will expect the best of everything. Service. Food. Décor. Amenities. And they will find it here. It will have an English motif. The name hasn't been chosen yet, but it will most certainly have British significance. The hotel will be small. It will boast 20 rooms and 10 luxury suites, each decorated to represent a particular English literary figure and each room or suite will have a selection of the books by that author. All improvements will be kept to the highest standards set by the National Registry of Historical Landmarks and everything will be as authentic as possible. We've studied the provenance of the present building. It was built in 1908. It will be representative of that era. Even bath fittings will be of the period, with mahogany encased tubs. Extreme care will be taken with craftsmanship. Do I have any questions so far?"

"Yes." An elderly woman raised her hand. She wore a dark purple, pantsuit. "Mr. Crawford. Won't this hotel bring a plethora of taxi cabs roaring into and out of the area?"

"We have plans for a fleet of automobiles to collect and return guests to and from the airports. These will undoubtedly be limousines. Then, we shall also have at least six Rolls Royces to be used by guests needing to be taken to appointments, theater outings, dinner and so forth. We anticipate taxi traffic to be kept to a minimum."

The lady in purple smiled and nodded.

Another lady spoke up. She was holding a small, white poodle in her arms. "Will guests be allowed to bring pets?"

"Yes, Ma'am. The hotel will be pet friendly. Pet sitters will also be available and no animal will be allowed to remain in a room alone. They will be walked at regular intervals. There will even be a pet grooming facility on the premises, as well as an upscale beauty salon. We'll even have an in-residence dog. Probably a Golden Retriever, in keeping with the English theme.

A heavy-set, older man stood up. Will you be using Union workers?"

"For the most part Sir. Some of the work calls for old world craftsmanship that is almost impossible to find. If we are unable to find Union workers with those skills, we will then go to unique, artisanal craftsmen. I hope that doesn't happen too often and we intend to negotiate with the Unions about this possibility." The gentleman smiled and resumed his seat.

At the conclusion of the meeting, it seemed that all questions had been answered and any concerns addressed. Wine was served and people circulated about, chatting with one another. Isabella spent her time describing ideas for the room décor. The women particularly seemed charmed. All in all, it was a successful afternoon and when Chris and Isabella left, they felt that a huge hurdle had been crossed off their list. Chris sent Sarah Childers-Long a sweet vase of mixed roses the next day.

The project began. Permits were acquired. Union negotiations completed and architectural blueprints perfected. It all went smoothly. As the months flew by, Chris and Isabella watched their dreams become reality. Room by room, floor by floor it took shape. Entering each room was like stepping back into the era it represented. The neighborhood's interest was piqued further when Chris and Isabella requested that the name for the hotel itself and for the two dining spots become the brainchild of the neighborhood association. After much deliberation and a silent auction, the name *Queen Anne* was chosen for the hotel itself. The grand dining room was to honor King George VI for his steadfastness during World War II and would be known as the George VI Room. It was a Renaissance revival style, featuring attached ionic columns and an elaborate coved ceiling. The smaller dining room was to be called the Queen Elizabeth Room and would be decorated on the order of an English sitting room.

The summer months rolled by and when Isabella and Chris weren't busy with the new Hotel, they found endless ways to enjoy each other in the wonder that was New York. They visited countless museums, attended Broadway plays, dined in small out-of-the-way bistros in the upper '60's and '70's. They danced to the music of The *Umbrellas of Cherbourg* on the roof of the St. Regis Hotel and enjoyed after-work cocktails at the Top of the Sixes on Park Avenue. One weekend, they rented a car and drove to Cape Cod, where they stayed at an old, charming Inn. But, even then, there were separate rooms.

Isabella had hoped to go home to England for the Holidays, but the work on the hotel was overwhelming and her presence was called for every moment. The same was true for Chris. Her parents were vastly disappointed, as this was the first time she had had to postpone a visit because of the *Queen Anne*. They even suggested that they pay a visit to her in New York, but she discouraged such a plan, as she knew that she would be so busy and wouldn't be able to give them the time and attention they deserved. So, she and Chris spent a quiet Christmas in New York. He put up a tree in his apartment and they decorated it together. It was fun spending their first Christmas together. There was no question that they were very much in love, and both had told the other as much. From the moment of their meeting, neither had seen another person of the opposite sex on a dating basis. And there was no question that both of them knew where the relationship was heading. Isabella knew that there was no way on earth that a man would spend the amount of time with her that Chris had, without so much as an attempted inappropriate move, unless he was serious. Sometimes she was sorry she had ever promised herself celibacy, but she had and she meant to hold true to herself.

When the tree was decorated, they poured another glass of eggnog, spiked it with some rum and sat down on the black, leather couch. Chris put some Christmas Carols on the tape player. Everything was lovely. Until the song *I'll be home for Christmas'* began to play, and Isabella began to weep.

"Oh, my sweet Isabella. What is it? Are you homesick? Does this song make you want to be at home?" Chris asked, concerned.

"I guess so," Isabella sniffled, through her tears. She tried to smile. It isn't that I'm not glad to be here with you. I just miss home at Christmas."

"Next year we'll be there for certain, I promise".

"Do you really think we'll still be together in a year?" she asked, with a watery smile.

"Isabella. I think we'll be together forever. Don't you?"

"I don't know. I haven't thought about it a lot. I guess so. But, someday I plan on returning to England for good. What then?"

"Then, I'll be returning to England too. It's good I never gave up my British citizenship," he smiled.

"Are you serious?"

"Yeah. I sure am. Kaplan has a big office in London. I can always ask for a transfer over there. I'd probably get it."

"But. You've always said that you love New York so. I didn't know you were thinking anything of the sort."

"I guess I really didn't know it either. But, I know I told you once a long time ago that I was never going to let you go. So, how can I let you move back to England alone?"

"Chris. What are you saying, exactly?"

"That I love you madly and want to marry you."

"Oh my God! Are you serious? Are you asking me to marry you?"

"No. I'm *telling* you that I'm going to marry you." He laughed. In fact, in order to wipe away those tears permanently, I think perhaps I should give you your Christmas present a little bit early." He walked over to a drawer in a chest in the foyer and took out a small box. It was obviously a jeweler's box. He handed it to her. "Here Isabella. I'm sorry it isn't wrapped. But, your tears messed up all of my plans."

She opened the top of the velvet covered box and there lay a spectacular two-carat marquis cut diamond ring, set in platinum. "Oh my God! Chris! I never expected anything like this! It's just so beautiful. Here, please put it on my finger, she said, holding out her left hand. He picked up the ring and slipped it on her lovely hand. It fit perfectly. Then, he took her in his arms and held her close before kissing her gently and passionately. "I love you, Isabella. Will you marry me?" he asked.

"Oh, yes, Chris, yes." She was crying again, but this time the tears were ones of happiness. Oh. What a wonderful surprise. I want to tell the world. We have so much to talk about, so much to decide. Shall we be married here in New York, or in England? How long do you want to wait? Do you want a large or small wedding? We can't even think about this until the *Queen Anne* is complete and open."

"Slow down. There will be time to work out all of the details. The only thing I agree with for certain is that we can't think about getting married until after the *Queen Anne* is open. Big or small, New York or England. None of that matters to me. You'll want to discuss all of that with your mother and father. The only think I'll add is that if we're to be married and are going to live in England, we might as well be married there."

"Oh, Chris. I'm completely overwhelmed. And so very excited. I never dreamed…Well, I *dreamed*, but you pulled the rug right out from under me. I thought maybe *someday*. They kissed again. "You know, it's getting harder and harder for me to say 'no'.

"Isabella. I won't let you give in now. I'm looking forward to a spectacular wedding night."

"I'd like to ring my parents, but then again, I think I'd rather wait and let them meet you, and then spring it on them. I know they'll think you're grand. Let's plan a trip to England right after the *Queen Anne* opens in the spring. It's so beautiful there at that time, too."

"That's fine with me, Isabella. But, can you keep our secret for that long? That would be about half a year."

"I know, but I really think I can. It would be such fun. They'll think I'm just bringing you home for a casual introduction and then I'll show them the ring. That way Mummy and I will be together and we can make a lot of plans while we're there. And, I want you to see the Chapel."

There was silence for a moment. "Oh Gosh, Chris! We've never discussed religion. I'm a very devout Catholic. You're Anglican. What do we do about that?"

"Obviously, I convert to Catholicism."

"You would do that? For me?"

"Not *only* for you, although I have to be honest and admit that I never would have considered doing so, if I'd never met you. I've done a lot of reading, comparing the two belief systems. They aren't *that* different. If I could live all of this time without any sex, I guess I can learn not to use birth control! Anyway, I'd really like to have a large family. How do you feel about that?"

"I would too. I hated being an only child. I really wish I'd had brothers and sisters. And, you were an only child too. So, I think we'd like to fill the house with little ankle biters." They both laughed. He reached over and put his arms around her.

"I love you so much, Isabella. I never dreamed I'd find anyone like you. You've turned my life upside down in just these few months we've known each other. I don't ever want to be without you."

She snuggled her head against his chest. "Oh, Chris. My parents always taught me that I would know when I met the right person. That he would be the one God meant for me. You're so obviously that person. I just know we're going to be so happy."

He never tired of running his fingers down her cheeks. They were just as smooth as he'd known they'd be when he first saw her. Everything about her was so perfect. He put his lips upon hers and soon they were holding one another in a tight embrace and kissing intensely. They lay down on the couch and she could feel that he was aroused. It was always that way when they let it get to this point and she knew it was time to call a halt to their passion. Yet, it felt so good and so right. He placed his hand on her breast and she didn't stop him. Soon he was caressing her thigh, as he moved her skirt up her leg. Still, she didn't stop him. Their kissing became even more intense. Chris unbuttoned her white blouse and reached his hand inside of her bra. She felt like she was on fire. They had never let it get this far before. They were both murmuring words of endearment and love. He slipped his hand inside of her panties and she felt a jolt of passion that she had never known. Suddenly, it was Chris who pulled back.

"No, Isabella, no. This isn't right. We swore this wouldn't happen. I want you more than I've ever wanted anything in my life, but we've both sworn to wait until we're married."

"Isabella was crying. "Oh, Chris. This is so much harder than I ever dreamed it would be. Perhaps I was wrong to promise I'd wait. Now that we're engaged. Well, that isn't so terribly different than being married."

He wiped the tears from her eyes. "Yes, it is, sweetheart. I made you a promise and I intend to keep it. It's the hardest thing I've ever done. But I also know it's what's right." He straightened her blouse and she sat up.

"Yes, I know you're right. Thank you for being sensible," she smiled, as she smoothed her skirt. The next months are going to be difficult, Chris. I'll try not to lead you on like that. I didn't mean to. I just got totally carried away. I love you more than I could ever have imagined."

"I understand. So did I. That isn't going to happen again. I promise."

Chapter Eight

MAY 6, 1965

*I*sabella and Chris held firm to their resolve and as the months flew by, their love continued to grow. They made wonderful plans for a summer wedding in England and counted the days until the *Queen Anne Hotel* opened, as they knew they would be traveling to England soon after. An enormous celebration was scheduled for May 6, 1965, in the hotel's ballroom. Everyone who was *anyone* in New York was invited and it was to be a spectacular event. Isabella hadn't dressed up elaborately since her father's knighting ceremony, now some years before. She decided to splurge on a wonderful gown, which she would keep for her honeymoon too. She chose a strapless, pale pink, silk chiffon, Jean Patou gown, with a heavy Venetian lace bodice. It was the most beautiful gown she'd ever owned.

She wore her hair in the upsweep that Chris adored and he gave her a pair of diamond drop earrings as a memento from the opening of the hotel. She felt like Royalty. When they arrived at the *Queen Anne*, Isabella was astounded. One would have thought that it was a movie premiere. There were even Klieg lights and a red carpet. She saw the Mayor, the Governor, every television personality from Barbara Walters to Geraldo Riviera, and every Hollywood celebrity from Elizabeth Taylor to Cher. Chris was dressed to perfection in white tie and tails. They danced the night away, and basked in the glory of the spectacular hotel that had resulted from their hard work and planning. They received telegrams from friends and relatives and Isabella's parents sent a beautiful arrangement of flowers.

When Chris arrived back at his apartment near four in the morning, there was a message for him to telephone his Uncle Gene. He assumed that it was more accolades regarding the spectacular achievement that was *The Queen Anne*. Chris hadn't spoken to Gene since the last time his uncle had been in New York City and he'd made every effort to put their conversations about Isabella out of his mind. He wished they had never discussed her. Shedding his jacket, he put through the call to London, after checking his wristwatch and making the assumption that Gene would be at work at eleven o'clock, which would be the time in England. Sure enough, Eugene answered on the second ring.

"Well, you've scored a tremendous victory, I hear," Gene said, when he realized it was Chris.

"You mean the *Queen Anne Hotel*? Yes, Gene, I'm very proud of how it all came together. It was a lot of darned hard work, but in the end it was all worth it. The hotel is really something to see. It looks like it's going to become *the* place for famous people. Of course, that doesn't really surprise me. It's out-of-the-way, so they have all of the privacy they want, and as luxurious as anyone can imagine."

"I understand that Isabella played a big part in the hotel's success, as well," Gene replied.

"Yes, she did. An enormous part. The entire concept was her idea and it's what makes the property so unique. Kaplan was fortunate to have her as the chief designer."

"And how are things progressing between the two of you?" Gene asked, in a rather coy voice.

"Great. We're wild about each other." Chris wanted so badly to tell his Uncle that they were engaged, but they had promised each other that they would wait to make the announcement when they reached England. Isabella didn't even wear her ring all of the time, for fear the word would get around, and somehow her parents would learn of their plans.

"So I gather," Gene said.

"How do you mean? What would you know about our relationship?" Chris asked, with a puzzled tone in his voice.

There is a giant photograph in yesterdays' *Times* of you and Isabella, standing in front of the *Queen Anne*. The article is about the new hotel, but it spotlights how the two of you were the brains behind it. It mentions Isabella as your fiancée."

"Oh Jeez! You're kidding. Who in the world gave them that story? We've never said a thing about being engaged."

"Well. Are you engaged?" Gene asked.

"If we were, I wouldn't tell you," Chris laughed, uncomfortably. "I've never even met her parents, you know."

"Well. *Yes*, you have, Chris. You just don't remember."

"Then, for all practical purposes, I've not met them," Chris retorted. Now, Isabella will have to phone her parents and tell them that the Press continually overdoes things, just to make a good story."

"I wouldn't worry too much about it. They'll believe whatever Isabella tells them. So, I'm wondering when I'm going to get my 'finder's fee' for putting you two together," Gene remarked.

"What? You're joking, I assume? And anyway Gene, you didn't put the two of us together. I met Isabella at a dinner at the Mayor's home. Remember?"

"Ah yes, Kippy…Chris. But, would you have known who she was, if we hadn't lunched the day before?"

"It wouldn't have made any difference if I'd known who she was. The moment I saw her, I was blown away."

"Yes, but I wonder if she would have been quite so intrigued with you if she'd known of our prior conversation?"

"What are you implying, Uncle Gene? I don't care one bit about Isabella's background, or about anything that went before. I've told you that."

"Well, I suspect that if she knew everything that we'd discussed before you met, she might take another look at whether she can trust you."

"Gene. Are you implying that you intend to tell Isabella about your harebrained scheme? You know that could cause no end of uproar. Why would you even think of doing that?

"Well Chris, I'm running a bit short on funds these days. The cost of living over here is out-of-sight. I could use some help from you. I know you're doing very well and I know that Lord Nigel Somerville settled a nice, fat inheritance on you when you turned twenty-one. Plus, if you end up marrying into the Somerville family, there will be no end to the riches you'll have access to. I think you owe some of that to me."

"Gene, this is unbelievable. I'd be happy to help you out with a loan, if you need it, but I really don't like your tone of voice, or what you seem to be hinting at. Are we going to have problems because of greediness?"

"Come on Chris. I don't call it greediness. Families should help one another out. I *am* the one who put you on to Isabella. I'd just like to have what I'm due."

"And, what do you think that amounts to?"

"Oh, I'd say a nice round half million pounds would do me nicely."

"Are you crazy? Even if I had that sort of money, why do you think I'd give it to you?"

"Because, if you don't, I'll have a chat with Isabella. I don't think there is any doubt that she'll believe what I have to say."

"Gene, you're a *bastard*. What you're talking about is blackmail, plain and simple. Isabella knows of the relationship between her family and mine. She knows her grandfather married my mother. It isn't of the slightest interest to her, except that it makes for interesting conversation about how we were undoubtedly meant to meet again later in our lives, as we have."

"Does she know everything, Chris?"

"What are you talking about?"

"About how you researched her at the New York library. About how you already had a copy of her debutante picture when you saw her at the Mayor's dinner?"

"No. She doesn't know that. Why would she? It's irrelevant. Gene, what you're suggesting comes about as close to blackmail as a person can get. Well, it isn't going to work, *Uncle* Gene. Now, I don't have anything more to say to you. I'm sorry I called."

Chris hung up the telephone. He was shaking all over. *Damn Eugene.* Chris should have been smart enough to realize that Eugene was working some scheme when he brought up the subject of his meeting Isabella. Even though he had flatly turned down his stupid idea, Gene *did* have information that he could tell Isabella. Would she believe him? It was hard to know. He wished now that he had told her on that very first meeting that he and his Uncle had been discussing her just the day before. He should just have been honest. Now, the whole thing could blow up in his face. *Should he tell Isabella now? If he did, wouldn't she wonder why he'd waited so long? Would she think that the only reason he was telling her was because Gene was trying to blackmail him? How would she know that it hadn't all been a plan for him to finagle his way back into the world of Lords, and Ladies and mansions like Willow Grove Abbey?*

Kippy broke into a cold sweat. It seemed that the best thing to do was ignore Gene's threats, go to England, meet Isabella's parents, and never speak to his uncle again. If he had to, he would lie about ever having had lunch with or seen his Uncle Gene when Gene was in New York.

On Memorial Day weekend, 1965, Isabella and Chris boarded a British Airways 747 and flew off into the night, on their way to Heathrow Airport in London. Shortly before boarding the plane, Isabella put a call in to the parents from the airport. She excitedly told them of the discovery she'd made that she and Kippy were related through the marriage of his mother and her grandfather. Her mother sounded stunned, and there wasn't really time to go over all of the details. She and Kippy had decided to give her parents a head's up about the relationship, before they landed in London. It seemed like a rather bug piece of information to drop on them without any warning. Isabella could see no reason at all why her parents should be upset. After all, it wasn't like they were blood relatives.

They had splurged on first class seats for the overseas flight and had a wonderful time, stretching out and ordering fine wine. Isabella chattered excitedly about seeing her parents after such a prolonged absence and about everything she had to tell them. Chris was a tad worried. He intended to carry through with his story that he had never known of or even heard the name Somerville, until Isabella told it to him. He'd never even met his step-father and Isabella scarcely had memories of his mother, her step-grandmother. He had to laugh at the idea of his mother being Isabella's step-grandmother. From what he remembered of his mother, she was not the grandmotherly type. The only thing he was worried about was whether Gene had followed through on his threats and might have rung Isabella's parents. There was such bad feeling between the two families that Chris wasn't even certain Sophia would speak to him if he did call. He hoped not.

The next morning, Chris and Isabella's plane set down at Heathrow Airport in London. They rented an automobile and within two hours they had arrived at *Willow Grove Abbey.* It was quite warm for May and Isabella was pleased, as Kippy would be able to see her home when the weather was not terribly dreary, as it often could be in England. When the two of them walked into the Great Hall, Sophia took one look at Chris, and knew beyond any doubt that it was Kippy. He still had the same boyish look she'd adored when he was a small child, and more importantly, he had Edwina's eyes, as well as a cleft chin. She remembered that Dieter had a cleft chin. The eyes were Edwina's blue-green, with the same expression. Of course, Spence had never spent the amount of time with Dieter as she had, so he didn't have a clear recollection, but he said that he could clearly see the resemblance to Edwina. It was a bit disarming to see those eyes. Sophia felt as though Edwina were back at *Willow Grove Abbey.* He had a very sweet smile, and was quite handsome, with blonde, rather longish hair, combed to the side. He was dressed impeccably in grey flannel trousers and a blue blazer and she immediately understood why Isabella was smitten

She took his topcoat, put it into the hall cupboard and they all went into the drawing room. Sophia could tell that Isabella was somewhat nervous and she remembered that terrible feeling. Wanting her parents' approval so badly and praying all would go well. There was no question that the entire scenario was bizarre, but, to coin one of Spence's favorite expressions, perhaps Kippy and Isabella's meeting was *serendipitous.* Isabella made the introductions and Spence shook Chris's hand, while Sophia gave him a warm hug.

"So, Isabella and Chris, how was your flight," Spence asked.

"Just fine, Sir, very smooth. We both slept most of the way. It's nice to be back in England."

"Is this the first time you've been back since childhood?" Sophia asked.

"Yes, actually. I was only about two when I left. I was away at Groton, when my Mother became ill."

"I'm sure you're tired after the long journey," she continued. "While we're anxious to get to know you better, I suspect that you would like a bit of a rest. Isabella, why don't you take Chris to his room, after he's had a cup of tea, or coffee. I know how dreadful jet lag can be. Awful."

"A cup of coffee would be nice," he replied. "I *am* a little bit worn out. A short nap will probably revive me. I appreciate your thoughtfulness."

"Not at all. Jet lag can be beastly."

Nan brought coffee for everyone, and they all chattered about inconsequential matters, until Chris set down his cup. His eyes were looking droopy. Isabella stood up, reached out her hand, and he took it.

They looked so very much in love and Sophia's heart turned over.

Please let everything be alright, she silently prayed.

"Come on then Chris," Isabella smiled, "Let's get you settled in. Mummy and Papa, why don't we plan on having tea together? Chris and I should be revived by then," she said, turning in their direction.

"Excellent," Spence replied. "I imagine it's been awhile since you've had a proper English tea, Chris. We'll make certain it's top drawer."

"That sounds wonderful, Sir," Chris replied. Then, he and Isabella disappeared up the stairway.

At four o'clock, they all met in the drawing room again. Chris had changed into a pair of casual khaki pants and another blue oxford shirt. He looked refreshed. Isabella was wearing a pale pink summer dress, with a lovely floral print. Nan had outdone herself preparing a sumptuous tea, complete with scones, clotted Devonshire crème, strawberries, pastry puffs, and cucumber and watercress sandwiches. They all helped themselves and Sophia poured the tea. Then they sat down and engaged in conversation.

"Then, Chris, where did you live in England?" Sophia asked.

"Well, you know, we were in London for the most part. I don't know where else."

Isabella interrupted. "Mummy and Papa Can you believe that Chris' mother was married to Grandpapa. Isn't that astonishing?"

"Well. Yes, indeed, it *is* rather astonishing. How long have you known this?"

"Well. Not very long after we met, I had tea with Lady Childers-Long. She's the one who told me. She knew Chris's name and knew that his mother was Edwina Phillips and that she'd been married to my

Grandfather! I couldn't believe it. Then, when I told Chris, he couldn't believe it either. It's like you always say, Papa. It was *serendipitous*."

"You didn't know the name of the man your mother had married, Chris?" asked Spence.

"I suppose I did, at one time. But, I really didn't pay much attention. I knew she'd married an Earl."

Chris wished they would stop asking so many questions. He hadn't been pre-pared for an inquisition. Of course, he'd expected that Isabella's parents would want to know more about him, but she'd never shown much curiosity, and he thought he'd covered all bases in his thinking about it ahead of time. He thought they'd be more interested in his education and the like.

"How did this tea come about, Isabella?" Inquired Spence.

"Well, I wanted her help with the neighbors who lived near her in Sutton Place, because we anticipated some difficulty with them regarding approval for the Queen Anne Hotel. I told her that Chris Crawford was working on the project with me, and she told me that she knew who Chris' mother was. I guess she was in London at the time. I was knocked for six! Then, I went back and told Chris and he hadn't even known it."

"Hadn't known that his mother was married to Nigel Somerville?" Spence asked, in a perplexed voice.

"No, Sir. I didn't. I knew she'd married an Earl. In fact, I knew his name was Nigel, but if she ever told me the last name, I don't remember it."

"Well that must have been quite a shock to the both of you," Spence continued.

"Yes, of course. You know, it's not the sort of thing that happens every day. No one talked to me very much about my mother. I guess they thought it would upset me. So, I knew very little about that part of her life."

Was it possible that he truly didn't know? Surely, he knew her true name? Something was not right. Spence and Sophia exchanged a quick glance. It was clear that they both felt the same way. Never one to mince words, Spence decided to come straight to the point.

"Chris, this is going to sound a bit cheeky of me, but I feel that some-thing is amiss here. I am almost certain that you are Kippy Phillips and we knew you as a child. Your full name is Christian, if I remember cor-rectly. The problem I'm having with this is that you inherited quite a large sum of money from Nigel Somerville when you turned twenty-one. Your Uncle, Eugene Phillips was the trustee. In fact, I was present when the papers were signed, giving you full rights to your inheritance. Someone from Nigel's family had to be. Surely you knew the name of the man who was so very generous with you?"

Chris put his cup of tea down and tried to look perplexed. "Well, yes. I *did* come into a rather large inheritance when I turned twenty-one." He swallowed hard several times and began to flush from his neck upwards.

"Kippy, something isn't right here. There is no way that you wouldn't have known that your mother had married the Earl Somerville. Simply no way. Not only was it on those papers, which dealt with the inheritance he left for you, the name would also have been on your mother's Will and death certificate, all of which you had to have seen. You weren't a baby then."

"Yes, I suppose I did see them. Perhaps I simply forgot," he said. It was a lame excuse.

"Kippy...sorry, Chris. I don't believe you're telling us the truth."

"Papa, what a rude thing to say to Chris. We planned on telling you all of this. Chris *did not* know the name Somerville. I'm certain of that. I asked him specifically about that."

"*Darling*, he had to. I simply can't accept that he didn't," Sophia responded.

"I didn't even know anything about *his* mother. Why didn't I know that she had married Grandpapa?"

Well, darling, you *did* know, Sophia added. "We didn't spend a lot of time dwelling on it with you, but you were at your Grandfather's funeral. Don't you remember his second wife? You were never around Edwina much during that time, but you knew her when you were very small. In fact, you and Kippy played together, when he was just a baby and you weren't much older. About three, I think. That was during the war, when your father was away and we were staying here at *Willow Grove Abbey*. Edwina stayed here too, for a time. "I'm sorry Chris," Sophia said, turning to him, "I'll try to remember to call you Chris. It's just that I've always thought of you as Kippy. Surely you knew your mother's correct name?"

"Well, of course I knew her name," he answered, completely chagrined.

"Quite. Why then did you tell us that you didn't know the name Somerville?" Spence asked, "and why did you just say that you had never heard mention of that name. What's going on, Chris?"

"Because…Because I hadn't told Isabella the truth about knowing of the connection between us, until she found it out from Sarah Childers-Long."

"*When* did you plan to tell me, Chris? You must have known who I was a long time before then?" There was real anger in Isabella's voice.

"Yes. yes, I did. However, I also didn't want to upset you. I knew that there were bad feelings between my family and yours. I was afraid that you wouldn't want to see me anymore, if you knew that my mother was Edwina Phillips."

"Don't you think I should have been the judge of that? Moreover, didn't you know me well enough, at some point, to know that I'm not like that. Why would it matter to me if Edwina Phillips was your mother, or my step-grandmother, or whoever the hell she was?"

"I don't know. I suppose I'd fallen in love with you and I didn't want to take a chance."

"So you chose to lie? Chris. Or Kippy. Or whoever you are. You are well aware of how I feel about lies. Anyway, I don't believe you. I think you're lying now. There's more to this that I don't know."

"Chris, I think you'd better come clean," Spence said. "Whatever reason you had for trying to hide the truth, it can't possibly be as bad as continuing with this charade."

"No sir, you're right," Chris admitted, still looking terribly embarrassed and rattled. "Um, well, first of all, I always preferred 'Kippy or Kip, actually, but in the States, it wasn't a popular name, so my aunt and uncle thought I should go by my given name, Christian. I'm…I'm just…I don't know what to say.

"When did you figure out who I was?" Isabella asked.

"I knew who you were before we met, Isabella."

"What? How on earth? How could that possibly be? We met accidentally. On the other hand, did we? What are you talking about?"

"Isabella," he said, reaching for her hand. "My uncle, Eugene Phillips, told me all about you. He considers that your family cheated me out of my inheritance. He thought that a way for me to repair the damage was to meet you. And perhaps to have…"

Isabella grabbed her hand away. "In other words, this was a scheme to get me to marry you, so that you could weasel your way back into the Somerville family and eventually into the ownership of *Willow Grove Abbey*? I *do* remember the lawsuit that ensued following your mother's death. I have just never given it much thought, but didn't Grandpapa leave *Willow Grove Abbey* to your mother, and then when she died, didn't she leave it in Trust to you, and my family had to sue to get it back? I remember that was right about the time I left for *Ashwick Park*." She was obviously near tears.

"My uncle told me that there was a lawsuit following my mother's death, brought by the Somerville family. As I understand it, my mother inherited *this* house, and she in turn, left it in Trust to me, with my Uncle Eugene as guardian until I reached adulthood. Nevertheless, your family fought my mother's wishes and my uncle lost. Thus, obviously, I lost too."

"It wasn't that simple, Kippy. We had no choice but to sue," Spence broke in. "Sophia spoke to her father shortly before his death and he told her that the house would be left to Edwina for her lifetime. *Willow Grove Abbey* was to revert to the Somerville children at your mother's death," Spence exclaimed.

"So, you're saying that my mother tried to cheat your family?"

"Kippy, I know that has to hurt you, but, yes, that's exactly correct. It *is* possible that she wasn't thinking clearly, as she was very ill and she may have forgotten her promise to my father. But, your Uncle Eugene knew very well what he was doing," Sophia answered.

"Had there been a falling out?" Isabella asked.

"I suppose you could say that," Sophia replied. "It was all so complex and difficult. It's very hard for me to explain everything that happened."

"Well, Mummy, I think you had *better* explain what happened. This is all very confusing. I cannot believe that I knew nothing about any of this." Isabella was angry and Sophia couldn't blame her.

"Isabella, there wasn't anything that you really needed to know. Edwina became involved with my father and it was very hard for me to accept. She changed a lot after our days together at school, when we were extremely close friends. Almost sisters. It placed me in a very awkward position. Can't you understand that?"

"Yes, but surely Grandfather had the right to marry whomever he wished, when Grandmother passed away. I don't see why you couldn't have tried to accept his choice."

"Isabella, I know that you're upset, but don't talk to your mother in that tone of voice. Edwina caused such grief and heartache in this family. Long before, she married your Grandfather, there was ample reason for your mother to be frantic over Edwina," Spence declared.

Isabella began to cry. "I think this is beastly. Chris, I cannot believe you've done this to me. What sort of an evil person are you? How could I possibly have thought I was in love with someone who would lie to me in such a fashion?"

"Please Isabella. I'm trying to sort it all out, as I sit here. What I did was wrong. I admit that. I'm not that sort of person and I think you know that. However, I thought that I'd been cheated. I didn't know that I'd fall in love with you. But, I did. You cannot doubt that. I am crazy in love with you. That changed everything. I would have told you the truth, but by then, it was such a mess and I was terrified I'd lose you."

"Well, guess what? *Kippy*, you *have* lost me," she sobbed.

Chris slumped back against the sofa. He looked terribly distraught and both Spence and Sophia couldn't help but feel sorry for him. On the other hand, he *had* done something horrific, and nothing could change that. Chris leaned forward, his eyes on the floor. He was clearly trying to regain his composure.

"Under the circumstances, I don't feel that I can stay here, under your roof. I need to speak with my own family members, who are obviously not on friendly terms with yours. I can't sit here and listen to my mother and my own family maligned. You can't expect me to sleep in this home, when the reality is that my mother intended it to be *mine!*" He stood up, and rushed from the room.

Isabella just continued to sob and everyone fell silent. A few moments later, Chris came down the staircase, carrying his luggage. The front door closed and there was the sound of his rented auto on the gravel drive. He left the house, without as much as a 'goodbye.'

Isabella, Spence and Sophia were left to deal with their own emotions.

"Dearest, he's obviously very confused about his feelings and isn't certain what to believe or who. His Uncle Eugene has put terrible ideas into his head. That doesn't entirely excuse what he's done. Lying to you. Lying to us. Dear God, Isabella, we wouldn't have hurt him, or you, for the world. But, what were we to do?" Sophia asked. "Of course, he's confused, hurt and angry." Sophia felt very unsteady and shaky. The whole scene had unnerved her greatly. All of her life, she'd tried so hard to give Isabella happiness and security, and now everything seemed to be falling apart. Her heart ached for her daughter. Isabella's eyes were swollen and red, and she was still sobbing. Sophia stood up and went to her, putting her arms around her daughter.

Chapter Nine

June 1, 1965

"Isabella, darling, where do you think he's gone?"

"I'm sure to London. Then, I really don't know. I'm not certain that he knows anyone else here. But, then, I really don't know much of anything, do I? Perhaps he'll go to whomever this bloody 'Uncle Gene' is," Isabella sobbed.

"Darling, Papa and I would have done anything in the world to have kept you from this hurt. It's surrealistic that of all the people in the world, you'd meet Kippy."

"I don't even know this 'Kippy' you keep referring to. I brought home a wonderful man named Christian Crawford, and now you say he's Kippy Phillips'. It's too much for me to take in. I loved him, Mummy. I loved him with all of my heart, and now everything is ruined. How could he have lied to me so?" She jumped up and ran to the stairway, sobbing.

Sophia began to weep, as well. "What do we do now, Spence?" She felt depressed and at a loss to make a decision about how to act next.

"We support Isabella and hope that somehow this can come to a good resolution. It was a terrible thing for him to hatch such a scheme, but you know, Eugene is such a lowlife that nothing surprises me. Kippy really seems like a decent enough chap and I suppose if one's family has filled one's head with stories of evil people cheating them, then this sort of thing can happen. In addition, remember, he'd not met Isabella yet, then. Perhaps he really *does* love her now. Darling, we'll get through this," Spence said, as he placed his arm around her in an attempt at comfort.

"But Spence, we're going to have to tell her about the possibility that they're blood-related. I don't see any way around it. He may return. I believe they honestly *do* care for one another and it's unlikely it will simply end, with no further interaction.

"Yes, I'm afraid there's no question that we'll have to bare it all," he answered.

Sophia sighed deeply and wiped at her tears. "I suppose you're right. We've weathered worse, haven't we?"

"Isabella will handle this. She's a strong girl, like her mother." With that, they rose and walked hand-in-hand up the staircase to their daughter's bedroom. Her door was closed and Spence knocked gently.

"Please just leave me alone," she called, in a pitifully sad voice.

"Darling, please let us come in and talk to you. We have some important things to tell you about this terrible mess. Things you really *do* need to know. Please, Isabella," Sophia implored.

They heard her footsteps, as she rose from the bed, where she had undoubtedly thrown herself in despair. She opened the door. Turning, she walked slowly back to the bed, and lay down upon it, with her face to the pillow. "What could you possibly have to say that would make any difference at this point?" She asked.

"I don't know that it *will* make any difference, Isabella, but there are details about this dilemma that we haven't told you and your mother and I think you should know them."

"So, there have been other lies?" she said, accusingly, raising her tear-stained face to them.

"There have been no lies, Isabella. There have been occurrences that your mother and I felt you would have been far too young to understand and that, in any case, didn't have any bearing upon you, one way or the other. You can be angry at us, if you wish, but you must understand that there is no way we knew you would ever become involved with Kippy... Chris."

Isabella just sat there on the bed, looking forlorn and Sophia felt as if she was still about five years old. She wished she could put her arms around her and make everything all right. However, she couldn't. In fact, when the rest of the story was told, things were going to get even worse. Therefore, instead, she took a deep breath and began to tell the story.

"Isabella, one of the reasons, among many, that I was so terribly upset when Kippy's mother married Papa is because Edwina had been involved in an extramarital affair with your Grandfather years before your grandmother passed away. It became a very sordid situation and caused havoc in this family. It's the reason that I still have no relationship with my brothers. Not that there weren't other problems. But that added to them. Terrible words were spoken during that time. I was so beastly upset when your Grandfather became involved with Edwina. One of the primary problems was that Edwina had her baby *after* the affair began, a good while after. There was no assurance that Kippy…Chris, wasn't my father's son."

Isabella started to speak, but Spence put his hand up, and said, "Please, let your mother finish, and then you can say anything you wish." She closed her mouth, but looked as if she were in shock.

"So, at several points along the way, I specifically asked Edwina if Kippy were my father's son. She refused to tell me. One time she said that she was absolutely certain that he was *not*, but then, another time, she said she would never tell me the truth. I asked my father, as well. He finally told me what I believe is the truth, as far as he knew it. He said that Edwina had 'relations' with her husband and with Papa on the same day, so that either of them could have been the father. He truly did not know and he said that Edwina didn't either. They'd tried to determine the true paternity by blood tests, but all of them, Kippy, Papa, Edwina's husband Dieter, and Edwina were the same type. So, no one knows for certain, to this day."

"Are you saying that I could be in love with *your* half-brother? My uncle? Oh my God in heaven! Things like this don't happen in the real world," Isabella cried.

"Isabella, wait," said Spence. "We don't think that's the case, but only since meeting Chris. You mother says he's the spitting image of the fellow Edwina married before the war."

"He *is*, Isabella. There's no question in my mind. He has Edwina's eyes, but other than that, he's really a copy of his father. I have absolutely no doubt now that he is Dieter's son."

"Dieter? That's scarcely a British name. Nor French," Isabella said, in a perplexed manner.

"No, Dieter was German. I suppose *is* German, assuming he's still alive. Edwina married him shortly before the War began. He lived in the same building as she, in Paris. Nevertheless, Edwina was involved with my father already, before she married Dieter. It continued afterwards. Then, when the Germans captured Paris, she escaped and left him."

Isabella was sitting up, with her hands covering her face, in a gesture of despair and disbelief. "Do you expect me to tell Chris this latest bombshell? It would kill him. It would prove that his mother was a tramp! Moreover, it presents us with the lovely possibility that we are uncle and niece."

Sophia frowned. "Unfortunately, I think that Chris needs to know of this. If there is even the slightest chance that he is Papa's son, well, then both of you are going to have to deal with it. I hate it, Isabella. You should never have had to deal with such hurt. Let's see how Chris feels after he has had some time to digest everything he's learned. I haven't any idea what a conversation with his Uncle Eugene will accomplish, because I'm afraid there's considerable animosity on Gene's part. On top of that, I don't believe that Gene even knows about what we've just told you. I don't think Edwina ever told any of her family *that* truth. Nevertheless, we'll deal with it, if need be," Sophia added.

"Well, obviously his Uncle Eugene is a *bastard*," Isabella cried. "He started this whole nightmare. Surely if Chris does speak to him, he'll be a bit skeptical of what he's told?"

"Does he know any of his other aunts and uncles? Besides Eugene? I never knew them well, but I suspect not all are as motivated by money and revenge as Eugene is. Moreover, perhaps Edwina was more honest with some of them. Someone may know the truth."

"I don't think he's ever met his other aunts and uncles. I mean, since he was a little boy. However, what do I know? I didn't think he'd ever met *any* of his uncles and aunts, besides the Crawford's, who raised him. I know that his grandparents are deceased. They have been for quite some time."

Sophia thought about Thelma and George Phillips, and felt badly that they, too, were gone. It was not a great surprise, of course, given how many years had passed since her last contact with them. She couldn't even remember the names of most of Edwina's sisters and brothers, besides Fiona and Eugene. She had never met the sister who had married Craig Crawford, moved to Greenwich, and became Kippy's mother.

"Isabella, I'm confused about something," Sophia went on. "How is that you and Chris have known one another quite a length of time and yet he supposedly didn't know that your Grandfather was the Earl Somerville? I would think that might have come up somewhere along the way."

"Well, obviously he *did* know. But, I cannot say that he lied to me about that, because we hadn't spent our time together talking about the past. We've been more concerned with the present and the future. Of course I knew the essentials, and so did he. I told him about my father, that he's a prominent psychiatrist, and about his investiture. And I told him about all of your achievements, Mummy, and about my beautiful ancestral home, but I never went into detail about heritage and all of that. I may have mentioned the name Somerville once, but I'm not even certain of that."

How interesting. What a difference a generation or two can make! During Sophia's entire life the only thing her mother ever thought about was ancestry, heritage and the gentry. What a refreshing change.

She leaned over and put her arms around her daughter. "I love you more than anything in the world, Isabella, and I would have done anything to keep this burden from you. But, let's be optimistic, and believe that things may still work out."

"How could I ever trust him again, Mummy?" she asked, her voice muffled because it was buried on Sophia's shoulder.

"It might be very hard, but trust can be rebuilt," she answered. She looked at Spence and knew that they were both thinking back to a time when he'd dealt with whether he could ever find it in his heart to trust Sophia again.

"I've had some experience with that sort of thing," Spence answered. "I can absolutely promise you that it is, indeed, possible to trust again, after something has happened to temporarily shake your confidence."

Isabella looked up and said, "Of course, I'm not going back to New York, Mummy and Papa, until this is settled. I may never go back. I haven't even told you yet that we're engaged."

"Oh, Isabella. When did that happen?"

"Last Christmas. We decided to wait and tell you when we came to England. We were planning on being married here in the late summer… planning on staying permanently. Chris planned to ask for a transfer to Kaplan Hotel's London offices."

"Oh, Isabella, How lovely. If only everything hadn't gone awry. We'll get through this ghastly time together. Please know that Papa and I are here for you, and that we'll do everything in our power to help you. And Chris, of course."

"Mummy?"

"Yes, Isabella?"

"It's all right if you call him Kippy. I sort of like the name. It fits him," she smiled, through her tears.

Kippy rang Isabella after a four-day silence. He told her that he was in *Bury St. Edmunds* and wanted to see her. Isabella was even more distraught than before, as she was frightened to death about telling him the entire truth about his mother and her grandfather, and the whole morass that had enveloped them. Of course, she wanted to see him and in the end they agreed that he would return to *Willow Grove Abbey.* He arrived late in the afternoon, still driving the rented auto. He was very polite and friendly when Sophia opened the door. She was relieved to see that he seemed quite relaxed compared with his demeanor when he'd departed. She kissed him on the cheek, and he apologized for his abrupt departure when last he'd seen her. She told him that she understood completely why he felt the way he did, and then excused herself, moving into the library, saying that she had some correspondence to catch up on. He and Isabella needed time to be alone.

Isabella and Kippy went into the drawing room and sat down. She poured them each a glass of wine, which she had chilled and waiting. She was extremely nervous. It was obvious that Kippy was as well. He began the conversation by apologizing.

"Isabella, please forgive me for acting like an ass. I guess I was just completely caught off-balance when it became obvious that your parents knew who I was. You have to admit that this is an unbelievable situation."

Of course," Isabella replied, and thought to herself how much more *odd* it could end up being before everything was sorted out. "But, Chris, you *knew* that all of this could come out. What were you thinking?"

"I don't know. I wasn't thinking very clearly, obviously. It all got out of hand, Isabella. All I can say is that I never dreamed I'd fall so completely in love with you."

"And if you hadn't, you're telling me that you're the sort of person would have married someone he didn't love for the sake of an inheritance, or revenge?"

"No. No. I don't think that's fair. I know it seems that way. And, I'll never know, will I? My Uncle really did a number on me. I can't tell you how enraged I am about this. I never want to see him again. I need to tell you that I beat the *holy crap* out of him. I don't think I'll be hearing from him again. Talk about using someone to further personal gains. I haven't told you, but the night after the *Queen Anne* opened, after I got back to my apartment, about four in the morning, I'd had a call from Gene. He'd left a message asking me to call him back. I figured it was about the Grand Opening, and I *did* phone him. That isn't what it was about. He tried to blackmail me. He told me to give him a half million pounds, or he would tell you about the conversation he and I had the day we had lunch, before I met you. He threatened to let you think that I'd agreed to go along with his insane scheme to meet and marry you, so I could get *Willow Grove Abbey* back."

"Well, it's one more layer to this entire mess. So what do you think this looks like to me?"

"The same way, I imagine. What can I say, Isabella? It was a dumb-ass thing to do. To even think of. I'm not that sort of person. I've said that before. But, this has been an excruciatingly confusing situation. I'm sorry. I'm so very sorry. I love you more than anything in the world. I'll do anything if you'll forgive me. I don't want this house, or your inheritance I just want you. I'll sign anything to that effect. Please believe me."

"I *do* believe you, but I'm still having problems with the fact that you really aren't the person I thought you were."

"How so? I've explained to you that I got caught up in Eugene's despicable lies. I felt uncomfortable just talking with him about such a sordid scheme. He convinced me that my mother would have wanted me to follow his stupid suggestion. That I would be avenging her."

"Oh Chris. Kippy. My God. The entire time we've been together you were pretending. Don't you understand that I can't help but have some serious trust issues with you?"

"Look, Isabella, nothing has changed about *us* and the way we feel about each other. It's kind of neat to know that we've known each other all of our lives, when you stop and think about it. I don't care anything about whatever problems your mom had with my mom. They shouldn't be our problems. I can see why she would've had a rough time accepting her best friend marrying her dad. Jeez, anybody would, I'd think. At any rate, the important thing is that we care deeply for one another. You know how much I love you, and I know how much you love me, and nothing and nobody can change that. You *do* still love me, don't you?"

"Chris, I love the person I thought you were. You don't seem to get it. You've been *lying* to me all of this time. I don't know what I feel at this point."

"Isabella, I've never lied about my feelings for you. I apologize for not telling the truth about my mother. I apologize for being such a jerk, and listening to Uncle Gene, but we've planned a future together. The whole reason I came to England was to meet your parents and hope to receive their approval, you know that."

"Yes, and they *do* like you, a great deal, but it isn't that simple. Why would you ever have agreed to such a sordid scheme with your Uncle?"

"Isabella, I never did agree to anything. My uncle started this talk about my having lost my true inheritance. I think he's always been very money motivated, although I didn't particularly think about that then. He made it sound like your family treated my mother horribly. He was ecstatic when my mother married your grandfather, because of his wealth, and all. I believed everything he told me. It made me angry. Can't you understand that?"

"I understand your anger, but I don't understand your underhandedness. I really am going to need some time to sort this all out, Chris."

He reached over and touched the engagement ring on her finger.

"Isabella, let's not let anything else stand in the way of our happ ness. I'm sorry I acted like a jerk. I love you, and want to marry you. Just say that you love me, and that you'll marry me," he pleaded. He was so filled with longing and fear that he was going to lose her. He brushed his blonde hair back from his forehead, which he always did when he was nervous. "Come on, Isabella! Don't make me sit here in suspense. You *know* want to marry you. We've talked about it enough times. Please believe me. I did not ever agree to his imbecilic idea. All I did was sit there and listen. Yes, there were moments when it made me angry to think that my mother had been treated so shabbily. But, that's all. I told him when I next saw him that I wanted no part of such a dumb idea. Those are the exact words I used. All I lied to you about was the fact that he and I ever had such a conversation."

"Oh Chris, I'm overwhelmed, not about your asking me to marry you, but by everything that's happened. I'm afraid. I'm afraid to start a new life with you without making certain that we've worked this whole thing out. I mean, there were some very harsh feelings between your family and mine. And, you yourself seemed very upset that this house, *my* family's home was intended for you by your mother."

"Oh Isabella, forgive me, but that's crazy. I've tried to explain it all to you. Are you implying that I'd still want to marry you as a way to get what I think should be mine?"

"No, of course not, but *some* people might think it."

"Who in the hell would think it? Who? No one *we* care about? Unless, you're telling me that *your* parents think that?"

"No. I don't believe that would cross their minds. They aren't like that. But, I don't know, I just feel like we should wait until we understand all of the facts about this mess. I don't mean we would have to wait a long time, but just long enough for it all to soak in. I'm not sure I even understand everything that's happened."

"What don't you understand? My mother and your mother were school friends. My mother practically grew up around your family and after your grandmother died, your grandfather ended up marrying her. Sure, she was a lot younger than he was, but that happens a lot. You know that. From what my adopted Mom said, my mother was pretty sophisticated and worldly. She lived in Paris a long time, you know. It makes sense that she might like an older man."

"Or did she just marry him for his wealth?" Isabella questioned.

"How the hell do I know? I think that's not giving her the benefit of the doubt. The mother I remember was a good person. She loved me a lot. I guess she loved me enough to want me to have a secure future. That's why the issue with the house. She wasn't destitute, you know. She was a very successful designer."

"I know that, Chris, but my grandfather was an Earl. Marrying him made her a Countess, and as far as the house was concerned, that may have been what your mother wished for you, but it wasn't what my grandfather wanted her to do. She went against his wishes, Chris. It wasn't right."

"Who knows what his wishes were? Maybe they talked about it and he died before he could legally change things."

"I don't think so. And, anyway, Chris, there's more to the story."

"Why do you say that? What more could there be to the story? If you know something, tell me."

"All right. I suppose you should know. I've no right to keep things from you. *The way you did from me*, I might add." She gave him a sideways glance.

"Well, I don't see what it could be, and frankly, I don't care. That was *their* problem. Why are you insisting upon making it ours?"

"Chris, I'd love for it to go away, too, but that's not possible. There were some really bitter feelings. Please. Listen to what I have to say. This is just so complex, Chris. It can't just be swept away and forgotten. There are a lot of aspects to this muddle."

"Such as?"

"Such as, the fact that the upset between my mother and your mother wasn't just about Edwina having become involved with my grandfather after my grandmother died. They had at least an eight-year affair, Kippy. Eight years! It ruined my grandmother's life. She was never the same after that. My grandfather brought your mother to stay at *Willow Grove Abbey* during the War, and they carried on an affair right here, in my grandmother's own home. Grandmamma found out. My own mother was there, and she was pregnant. She and your mother had a huge row. Mummy ended up miscarrying. As a result, she could never have more children."

"Jeez, I'm surprised your mother will even speak to me."

"She doesn't blame you for these things. Neither does my father But, you need to know them, and there's more."

"What do you mean, more?"

"Kippy, your mother led my parents to believe that you were Grandpapa's son. I don't know how else to say that. *My* mother asked her over and over, on numerous occasions, if you were her half-brother and your mother wouldn't tell her. She even asked my grandfather. He said he didn't know."

"How could he not have known?" Kippy asked his face ashen.

"Because. Because, apparently your mother had sex with both my grandfather and the man she was married to on the same day."

Kippy jumped up and began to pace up and down the room. "Well, this is just... *fucking* unbelievable. This really can't be happening," he said. "I feel like we're in some sort of bad movie. The upshot of all this is that it's possible that I'm your uncle. Isabella, that's just plain insane. That couldn't happen in a million years." He shook his head, and ran his hands through his hair, in the endearing way that always made Isabella want to hug him. He looked perplexed and confused. "*Could it?*"

She looked at him with tears welling up again in her eyes. "Yes, it could."

"My God!" he shouted. "I don't know how I'm supposed to act. First of all, my mother is accused of being no better than a whore. Am I just supposed to accept that fact? Well, I can't. I don't believe she was like that." He was terribly agitated and seemed to be vacillating in his feelings. "I want to hold you in my arms and kiss you and tell you that I love you, and now I'm wondering if that would be incestuous. Jesus, Isabella, what can I say? It's *my* mother whom everybody is saying rotten things about. I loved her. She was beautiful and loving and I'm tired of having her name dragged through the mud!" he shouted, even louder.

"I understand that, but you need to understand that it's been a big shock to *me, too.* Also, I need to tell you that my parents, at least, are certain that you are *not* my grandfather's son. My mother knew your mother's husband. She says you look exactly like him, except for the color of your eyes."

"What do you expect them to say? If I were the Earl's son, I'd have some pretty strong reason to re-open the contest about the estate," Kippy answered, through clenched teeth.

"There, you see," Isabella sobbed. "Oh my God. I cannot believe you just said such a thing. Do you think that they'd take the chance on having their daughter marry someone who could be blood-related? It would be more likely that they'd say that they thought you *are* my grandfather's son."

Kippy knew that she was right, but he was in shock and confused, and everything was turning out all wrong.

Chapter Ten

June 7, 1965

"Kippy, can we please try to calm down and think this through, rationally?" Isabella implored. "Have you any information about your real father? You never have seemed to know much about him."

"Well, I know a little bit." He lowered his voice, resumed his seat on the sofa, but was clearly still terribly undone. "No one in the family knows much. Your parents knew more than my family. My father was a German, from Hesse Darmstadt. He was living in Paris when my mother married him. He was in the military, assigned to the German Embassy. Supposedly, they were married. When the war broke out, he was called back to Berlin."

"My mother told me that much," Isabella replied. "I think his name was Dieter, but she didn't say what his last name was. Obviously, it wasn't 'Phillips'. Why do you suppose your mother put 'Phillips' on your birth record, which you've told me she did."

"His name was *Schoen*. I hate it. I'm glad she chose 'Phillips.'" In spite of the seriousness of the subject, Kippy couldn't help but smile and Isabella suppressed a giggle.

"Anyway, yes, my uncle says they were married. He'd have no reason to lie about that. I don't know why she wouldn't have had his name on my birth certificate. Maybe she already knew she was going to leave him. I was born the year after the war began, in 1940. Perhaps she didn't want me to have a German name, because of the war. Maybe that's why they got a divorce?"

"It's possible, since I'm sure Germans weren't terribly popular in England and she was bringing you back here," Isabella answered. "Is there any way that you can get records, or would they be hard to come by for that period?"

"I don't know, but I'm going to look into it," he answered, through clenched teeth.

"Oh, this all just seems so unfair. Why couldn't you just be some great chap I met in New York, with none of this other baggage attached?"

"Ah, damn it, Isabella, who knows why things happen the way they do? I've always believed that things are meant to be, and that there's a reason for everything, but it's very hard to know what that reason is sometimes. The important thing is that we need to learn the truth, Isabella. Some way, we have to find out who my true father was, but I've no idea where to begin."

Kippy may not have had any idea where to begin, but Sophia did. Having grown-up with access to government sources most people wouldn't have had, she contacted a long-time Member of Parliament, and explained that her family had an urgent need to learn what had become of a German Officer after the war. She told him that in addition, she needed to know whether the Officer had ever married an English woman in Paris, and if so, whether they had divorced. Also, if he was still living, where could he be found? Her government contact took all of the relevant information and said he would do some investigation. He told her that he would be in touch with her. More than a week passed, while Isabella and Kippy stewed and fretted. Kippy stayed on with them, but the atmosphere in the house was tense, to say the least.

Kippy tried to learn more details about his 'father,' but made little headway. He contacted various Phillips relatives, but none had the slightest knowledge of Dieter. Isabella explained to him about her mother's contacts, and that news brought about more optimism than anything else since the entire ordeal had begun. He had no idea what he might learn from the man who might or might not be his father, but it *did* seem well past time that he knew the truth. Of course, he also had to face the very real possibility that the man might be dead.

Finally, Sophia received a return call from her government source. He imparted some vital information. He reported that shortly before the outbreak of World War II, the National Information Office in Berlin W 30, in accordance with Article 77 of the Geneva Convention, opened *The Wehrmacht Information Office for War Losses and P.O.W.'s*. In addition to providing information about foreign prisoners-of-war, its main tasks were the registration of German Wehrmacht casualties, wounds, illness, deaths and M.I.A.'s and the processing of these cases including personal status control and official grave service. The permanent personnel record for all soldiers was also available.

On June 14, 1946 the Allied Control Commission decreed that the WASt was to continue its work created by national and international commitments. At the same time the French section of the Control Commission took over the administration of the WASt. Sophia's British official had contacted WASt and was able to learn a good deal, in a wonderfully expedited manner. From him they learned that Dieter had served in the German Army, during which time he was an artillery Commander or Höhere Artillerie-Kommandeure (Harko). He had been wounded at The Battle of the Bulge. Through other sources, they learned that he had resumed his post-war life in Hesse-Darmstadt, but had eventually relocated to Lausanne, Switzerland, where he still lived quietly, in a small villa on Lake Geneva. Therefore, the wonderful news was that Dieter was still living and they had located him.

The decision was made for Isabella to accompany Kippy to Switzerland to meet his father. Boarding a morning flight, they made their way to Zurich where they transferred to a smaller plane, which took them to Geneva. In Geneva, they boarded a Lake steamer, crossing Lake Geneva lengthwise, and arrived in Lausanne, Switzerland in the late afternoon. Both were exhausted, yet exhilarated. The idea of finally meeting Kippy's father was overwhelming. They'd made reservations at the Beau-Rivage Hotel and wearily they made their way up the pathway from the Lake to the magnificent hotel, which overlooked the sparkling water. This splendid retreat had opened in 1861, and was known as one of the loveliest hotels in all of Europe. Isabella and Kippy could see why. Their two-bedroom suite had French doors that opened to a terrace, looking out onto Lake Geneva.

Each of them had a separate bedroom and they shared a common parlor-area. There, they were able to meet and either enjoy the terrace or have a private conversation in the elegance of a French inspired drawing room. They sat down together in that room and Isabella picked up a telephone book from the desk. She began to thumb through the pages, searching for Dieter Schoen's name. Sure enough, there it was! Kippy's heart speeded up as Isabella handed the book over to him. He jotted down the number and the address. Then, he walked over to the mini-bar in the room and took out two half-size bottles of wine. Smiling at Isabella, he poured each of them a glass. "I think I need a little fortification for this," he laughed wryly. She smiled in return and agreed with him. He walked to the desk, and picked up the telephone, dialing the number for Dieter Schoen. It rang several times before a female voice answered and in French.

"Bon jour. Ce la Schoen residence."

"Oui. Parlez-vous Anglais?" Kippy asked.

"Oui. Un peau. A little. How may I help you?"

"Is Mr. Schoen at home?"

"Oui. Yes. I will bring him. One moment."

There was a period of silence and then a man's voice came on the line.

"Ja. Dad ist Dieter Schoen. Wer ruft bitte?"

"Sprechen sie Englisch, Sir?" Kippy asked in German. He was so glad he had been brought up to speak several languages.

"Ja. This is Dieter Schoen. Who is calling please?"

"My name is Kippy Crawford, Herr Schoen. I am Edwina Phillips' son."

There was another significant pause. Then, in rapid German, "Edwina Phillips Sohn? Wer ist dein Vater, bitte? Edwina Phillips war meine Frau. Wir waren 1939 in Paris geheiratet. Wie alt sind Sie? "

"Please, sir. I do not speak or understand German that fast"

"Ah. Ja. Sorry. You say you are Edwina Phillips' son? Who is your father, please? Edwina Phillips was my wife. We were married in Paris in 1939. How old are you?"

"I was born in May, 1940. I think I may be your son. I know this is a shock. But, I am in Lausanne, and I want very much to meet you and talk with you. Would it be all right if to come to your home?"

"Ja. Of course. I should like to meet you. Do you know where I am located?"

"Yes. I have the address here. Would you object to my bringing my fiancée with me?"

"No. No. That is fine. When shall I expect you?"

"Um. Would eight o'clock be all right? We've just arrived and would like a rest and a bite to eat first."

"I'll expect you about eight o'clock then. Thank you for calling," Dieter said.

"Thank you, Sir. We shall be there at eight. Goodbye."

"Goodbye, Mr. Kippy."

Kippy replaced the receiver and gave a huge sigh. "Oh brother. He really sounds German. God. I can't believe I have a German father."

"Kippy. The war was over a long time ago. Was he nice?" Isabella asked.

"Yes. Very. I think I shocked him."

"Undoubtedly."

"Well, we have four hours. Do you want to rest, and then have dinner?"

"Yes, a lie-down would be nice. Why don't you wake me in about an hour? Then I'll have a bath and dress."

"Great. I'll see you at five." Kippy gave her a light kiss on the cheek. Ever since he'd learned that they could be uncle and niece, he had been much less affectionate. Of course, Isabella understood why. She felt the same way. Turning, she left the parlor, and went into her own bedroom to have a lie-down.

At five o'clock Kippy woke her. She really hadn't slept soundly, just a restless nap. *How was this meeting going to change their relationship?* She wondered. Isabella got up, and ran a nice bath. She rummaged through the few items she had packed, and decided to wear a simple crème-colored silk dress, with long sleeves and black piping at the jewel neckline. She twisted her hair into a long strand, and pinned it up, into a knot on top of her head. Then she slipped into a pair of black patent heels, and went out to the parlor to meet Kippy. He was waiting for her, dressed in a dark suit, with a white shirt, and blue striped tie.

"You look lovely Isabella. As always," he said, as he helped her with her coat. Usually he would have kissed her on the neck or cheek. She thanked him and returned the compliment, telling him that he looked wonderfully handsome.

Neither of them was hungry, probably due to nerves. They decided to wait until after their meeting with Dieter before they got something to eat. They left the suite and went out to the lavish entryway. Several taxi cabs lined up in front. Kippy flagged one, and the driver exited, holding the back door open. Isabella got in and slid across, so that Kippy could sit beside her. Then, Kippy gave the driver the address for Dieter's home and the car drove off into the night.

The house was located in the heart of what was called the Vaud countryside and was about thirty minutes from the inner city of Lausanne. When they arrived at the home, its appeal was striking. They later learned that it had been built at the beginning of the Nineteenth Century, and designed to assuage the owner's love of nature. It stood on a splendid plot of what looked to be at least several acres graced with fruit trees and a horse ring. Nature appeared to be left to its own devices, with any human intervention remaining discreet. It was especially pleasant in summer, and emanated a calm, convivial atmosphere. An outbuilding and a garage stood on either side of the main house. The garage doors were open and Kippy and Isabella could see two Mercedes Benz automobiles: A black sedan, and a small, white convertible. A few yards away were the garden and a stable.

The driver pulled up in front of the home, and Kippy and Isabella got out. Kippy paid the driver and he roared off. They approached the front door with anxiety and trepidation. Before they had a chance to knock, the door was opened and a traditionally uniformed European maid greeted them.

"Yes. I have been waiting for you," she said, with a French accent. "You are Mr. Kippy Crawford?"

"Yes. And this is my fiancée, Miss Isabella Stanton," he replied.

"Good evening, Miss Stanton. May I take your coat?" she asked.

"Yes, thank you," Isabella responded, while admiring the inside of the house. They were standing in a foyer. It opened into a living area of enormous proportions, spread over two levels. The ground floor, where they were, had a spacious lounge-dining room, enhanced with a splendid fireplace, and beautiful dark beams, as well as a functional kitchen whose white walls reflected brightness. Later, when Dieter showed them the rest of his home, they saw the upper level, which boasted a warm parquet floor and had four spacious bedrooms, two bathrooms and a game room whose many windows afforded a bucolic view of the fields and the garden. There was also an equipped terrace and some beautifully fitted out little corners which allowed one to take full advantage of the quiet, green environment. It was clear from the outset that Dieter Schoen was a man who enjoyed solitude and privacy. Perhaps the war had something to do with that.

The maid took them into the lounge area, and told them to make themselves comfortable. There was a fire roaring in the fireplace, even though it was a June night. But, in spite of it being a warmer time of the year, the fire felt cozy as the night held a bit of a chill. The marble topped, square table in front of the leather couch held a tray filled with tantalizing hors d'oevres, which made Isabella and Kippy suddenly ravenous. Kippy helped himself to some brie cheese which he spread on a water biscuit and Isabella did the same with a lovely arrangement of Liver Pate, served in a martini glass, with capers and chopped egg. There was an open bottle of white wine on the table, with two glasses. Kippy poured one for himself and one for Isabella. Then, they settled back and enjoyed the atmosphere of the unusual home, waiting for Dieter to appear. It didn't take long.

In less than five minutes, a good looking, older man entered the room. He had the same very blonde hair that Kippy had, just slightly thinner and somewhat receding. Isabella would have known him anywhere. He might have been Kippy in thirty years. His face was the identical shape of Kippy's: square jawed, cleft-chinned and thin lipped. The only distinct difference between the two of them was their eyes. Kippy had been blessed with his mother's eyes. A blue-green, that was almost turquoise. They were light eyes, topped with very long lashes. Dieters were very blue, like the Pacific Ocean, deep set and penetrating. Aside from that, there was very little difference between the two of them. Both were tall, although Dieter was quite thin. He did not look well. He had a pronounced limp in his right leg, but very erect posture. Isabella couldn't help but think it was a holdover from being a German officer. She kept waiting to hear him click his heels. There could be no question whatsoever that Dieter Schoen was Kippy's father and Isabella's heart soared. If that were the case, then both she and Kippy could stop worrying that they were related. Still, as certain as she was, she wanted desperately to hear the entire story of how and why Dieter had not known about Kippy.

When he entered the room, Kippy stood and Dieter approached. Dieter shook Kippy's hand. He seemed mesmerized and had difficulty taking his eyes off Kippy. It had to be apparent to him as well, that the resemblance was remarkable. "So. You are Edwina's son," Dieter remarked, as he held Kippy's hand for a moment longer and then, letting it loose, settled himself into a chair across from the couch. "I suppose I don't need to tell you how completely astonished I am?"

"No, Sir. I'm feeling the same way. I think there can be little doubt that you are my father. We look so very much alike. I don't mean to be impertinent, but did you know that my mother was pregnant when you last saw her in Paris?"

"No. Not with certainty, but I had my suspicions."

"Could you please explain it all to me? I've waited such a long time to know who my father is, and how it all came about."

"I'll be happy to. But, first tell me how you came to find me here, and what has brought you now, after so many years?"

"It's a very long, and somewhat strange story. I'll try to start at the very beginning and if I'm telling you something you already know, just tell me to stop."

"That's fine. I know very little, really."

"All right. Well. I was born in May of 1940, just a month before Paris fell. I guess you were back in Germany by then."

Dieter nodded.

"My mother was terrified and was able to arrange for high level help to assist her in leaving Paris and returning to England. Did you know Lord Nigel Somerville?"

"I met him once in England, when I was a guest at his home for a dinner party. It was a very unfortunate event. I was a young, brash, foolish man, with all of the dreams of glory and victory that so many young Germans had in those days. It was before the war, but Hitler was fast gaining fame. Of course, I thought he was a God. I made some very foolish remarks at the dining table and caused a terrible uproar. I was there with Edwina, but she refused to leave with me. She stayed on at Lord Somerville's home and I returned to Paris. I was an attaché to the French Embassy at the time. At any rate, I don't believe I ever met him again, although I know he was the father of Edwina's best friend."

"Yes. He was. Edwina's friend was Sophia Somerville. They roomed at school together in Kent, England. She is Isabella's mother."

Dieter looked perplexed. "You mean to say that you are engaged to be married to your mother's best friend's daughter?"

"Yes. Well, it's much more complex than that. I assume that you had no idea then that Edwina was involved in a romantic relationship with Lord Somerville?"

"Good God, No. When did that happen?"

"I'm sorry to say that it apparently began during that visit you spoke of a moment ago, when she was in England with you and stayed on at the Somerville home."

"But, Edwina and I reconciled after that."

"You may have, but she never ended her affair with Nigel Somerville."

"Was she seeing him while we were married?"

"I'm afraid so. In fact, it's that which has caused so much trouble, beyond the obvious. When Edwina discovered she was pregnant, she said she didn't know whose baby it was. She said it might have been yours, or it might have been Nigel's. No one has ever known, including me. Although, I didn't know any of this until quite recently. Isabella's parents knew it, and when they learned we'd met, fallen in love and become engaged, they felt they had to be honest with us, which of course, they were."

"Of course."

"Isabella and I met in New York City, where we have both been for a few years. We met through a business project. We knew about the connection between our families, between Edwina and Sophia, but not the rest. Anyway, the affair between my mother and Lord Somerville continued for many years. Finally, his wife, the Countess, found out. My mother, Edwina, was living at the Earl and Countess's home *Willow Grove Abbey*, as the Blitz had made it impossible to keep on in London. When Countess Pamela found out about the affair, she nearly killed Edwina. Edwina would not tell her whether I was her husband's son or not. So, my mother left and took me to America. I was just a baby. I never came back to England. When Sophia's mother died, my mother returned to England and married Nigel Somerville. Then, he became very ill and died not too long after. He left her the palatial estate and all of the money. I won't get into the nightmare that ensued. Suffice to say my mother did not do what she had promised her husband she would do. She died only a year or so later and did not return the property to the Somerville children, but left it to her brother Eugene."

"Ah yes. The scoundrel Eugene."

"You knew him then?"

"Yes, he borrowed thousands and thousands of pounds from me. Always looking for money, that one."

"Well, he tried to blackmail me into giving him a half million pounds for him to keep quiet about a conversation he and I had about Isabella. He wanted me to meet her, sweep her off her feet, and marry her, so that I could once again have a chance at owning *Willow Grove Abbey*. That isn't what I did, but I was afraid he would tell her that, and I would lose her."

"My God, what a disgusting piece of filth."

"Anyway, back to my mother and you. When she died, she'd never told who my father was. I think by looking at the two of us, anyone would know in a minute that we are father and son, but I would like to have more concrete proof if possible. Do you know anything that would help to clear this up?"

"I think I can clear it up very quickly. What a despicable thing for your mother to have done. I knew that she could be devious and sly, but I never would have dreamed she would have done this. Let me take you back to the months just before Paris fell. In the late summer of 1939, I was given a furlough of three weeks. I was virtually certain it would be the last I would receive for a long time to come. The rumor was that war would be declared in September. A friend of mine had a villa in Tuscany. He offered it to me so that Edwina and I could spend my furlough there, uninterrupted. We traveled there by train on the 2nd of August 1939. It was a Friday. Edwina had her monthly curse the week we left. When it was over, we made love almost continually from then until we left on August 23. She would have been due to have another curse at the beginning of September. I remember distinctly that it did not come, because on the 3rd of September war was declared. I knew I would be going back to Berlin, because the embassy in Paris would be closing. I didn't leave until two weeks later and still there had been no sign that she was not pregnant. I even spoke with her about the possibility, but she said she had always been very irregular and not to worry. But, I had known her a long time by then and I had never known her to be so much as an hour late. Since we were married when we went to Italy, no precautions were used. If you were born in May, Kippy, then I am one hundred percent certain that I am correct. She was pregnant when I left for Berlin."

Isabella suddenly jumped up and put her hand over her mouth.

"What's the matter, sweetheart? Are you ill?" Kippy asked with concern.

"No. I'm sorry. I just remembered something. Mummy told me that she spoke with Edwina the night war was declared, on September 3, 1939, and that Edwina had whispered to her that she was pregnant, but that she didn't intend to tell Dieter before he left for Berlin. That fits exactly with what you're saying."

"I think we can pretty well put this mystery to rest, "Kippy said, putting his arm around Isabella and kissing her on the cheek, as he used to before they'd known about Edwina's lies.

"Edwina was a very odd girl," Dieter continued. I don't want to hurt you, Kippy, but she was different. I loved her very much and thought she loved me too. But, obviously, I was badly mistaken. I wonder if she really ever loved anyone, except perhaps you, and herself."

"I'm not even certain of that anymore," Kippy answered. "But Dieter… is it all right if I call you Dieter?"

"Or Papa. Or Father. Whatever you would like," Dieter smiled.

"I called my adoptive father 'Dad' so let me try 'Father' with you," Kippy smiled. "What I was going to ask, *Father* is for you to tell me more about you. Since there seems to be no more question about my paternity, I'd really like to fill in some gaps. I know almost nothing about you."

"Ah Ja. I was born in Hesse Darmstadt in 1915. My family was always in the Diplomatic Corps. My father was an Ambassador to Denmark. I had two brothers, both killed in the war. My parents are also deceased. I was educated at the University of Heidelberg, and then in Vienna. I speak German, French and of course, English. This part of Switzerland is French, you know. I joined the military in 1937. I was posted to Paris as an attaché at the French embassy, with help from family connections." He laughed. "It was there I met your mother. We lived in the same building. I thought she was very beautiful. So much so, that she was the primary reason I learned to speak better English. We had happy times. I was young and foolish. I believed everything wonderful about the Third Reich. Hitler, of course, was a genius in my eyes. I was a fool. So were many of the young men my age. I'm lucky to be alive. Many who thought as I did aren't. Hitler! Acht! He ruined our beautiful land. He killed people for no reason. We never knew those were his intentions. *Damned, horensohn, arschloch, Mother Fucker.* I am sorry. I get upset when I speak of those times.

Edwina and I married, and I loved her very much. But, I think I always knew that there was something amiss. I don't believe she ever loved me. I suspected affairs. Even if the war hadn't come, I think our marriage would not have lasted. So, I left to go back to Berlin. I never saw her again. I would write to her, and the letters would return. At first she answered, but only a short while. I figured she had found some way to return to England. I thought that if I lived through the war, I would find her and we would resume our lives together. I *did* try after the war, but she was nowhere to be found. That is when I spoke to Eugene for the last time. He wanted money to tell me where she was. I had no money. No one in Germany had money. And even if I had, I would never have given it to him. I gave up and secured a divorce on grounds of desertion. I returned to Hesse Darmstadt after the war, and lived there until my parents died. Then, I chose to relocate here to Switzerland. A peaceful land. I never re-married. The war was so horrific, that I have been content to live here with my horses and land, flowers, and books. If I'd known of you, Kippy, of course I would have searched the world over. Eugene had to have known about you, yet he never told me a thing. Bastard! He robbed me of years with my own son."

"I understand how you feel, Father. I feel the same way. Oh, I wish we could make up for the years that were wasted."

"When are you and Isabella going to be married?" Dieter asked.

"As far as I'm concerned, as soon as possible," Isabella laughed. We came awfully close to losing one another. I'm sorry Kippy, but I'll never forgive your mother for her terrible deception. It was cruel."

"Yes, it was. Apparently, I never really knew her. I can't imagine abandoning someone like she did my father, and never telling him he had a child. And, of course, this nonsense about not knowing who the father was is just so much foolishness. She knew. She just hoped that she could convince Nigel Somerville that I was his child and persuade him to adopt me."

"Well. It's over now, thank God", said Dieter. We have to look ahead. Hopefully there will be some good times still to share." He got up and walked to where Kippy was sitting, with his arm still around Isabella. Dieter extended his arms, and embraced Kippy. "*Son. I have a son.* I don't deserve such happiness."

Kippy returned the embrace. "Yes. Yes. We both do. I'm so happy to finally have a real father. My adoptive father was a wonderful man, but I have always wondered who gave me life."

"When did your mother die?" Dieter asked, stepping back from Kippy.

"Quite a long time ago now. In 1949. She had lung cancer."

"Ahhh. Interesting. I, too, suffer from lung cancer. It was those disastrous cigarettes that we all smoked like candy in the 1920's and 30's. Of course, as a soldier, I was never without one. I remember that Edwina smoked continually too."

"Oh Father. No! You can't be saying that you have a serious illness. We've just found one another again."

"I'm afraid so, young Kippy. I am getting good treatment. Switzerland has some very good clinics. But, the outcome is pretty well established. I'll live another year. Perhaps two."

"Would you like to come to England and be with me during the time you have left?"

"I don't believe so, Kippy. I greatly appreciate such an offer, but I have my home, and my horses, and my little dogs. My servants take very good care. It would be difficult to make such a transition now."

"I understand that. But, I can't bear the thought of losing you, when I never really had you in my life."

"Sometimes life is very unfair, Kippy. But, I am a believer, and we shall meet again. Let's concentrate upon the immediate future. I should love to be able to be present at your wedding, Kippy. Do you think that's possible?"

"We will make certain that it's possible, Father. I promise you that."

Chapter Eleven

Night, June 7, 1965

Kippy and Isabella returned to the hotel. Both felt as though they had been through a terrible storm, but finally had survived. There was so much to discuss and it was hard to know where to begin. It was past ten o'clock and they decided they would order room service for something to eat, since they had skipped dinner. Now they were both ravenous. They spoke very little on the ride back to the Beau-Rivage. There was so much to say, so many plans to make and still so much to sort out. They held each other's hands in the back seat of the taxi and smiled at one another. The worst of their fears was behind them. They were not related. They arrived at the hotel, entered the front doors, and went directly to their suite, which was on the ground floor. Kippy shed his suit coat, and Isabella hung up her outer coat in the cupboard. Kippy opened the bottle of wine that was waiting on ice in the room and poured a glass for each of them. Then, they sat down on the sofa and heaved a sigh of relief.

"Kippy, I feel as though I've been through some sort of battle."

"I know. I do too. I can't believe we've found my father. I'm really, really glad about that, but I feel terrible about his being ill. *Damn*. It never seems like anything turns out perfectly, does it?"

"No, I guess not. But, the most important thing now is that we keep our promise to make certain he can be at our wedding."

"Do you think we ought to consider being married in Switzerland?"

"I hadn't thought of that possibility. That might be kind of neat and special."

Isabella picked up the telephone book they had discarded earlier, after finding Dieter's telephone number. She began to look for churches. Kippy made it easier. He called down to the desk and asked if there was a nearby Catholic church, where English was spoken.

"Yes, Sir. The closest would be The Cathedral of the Sacred Heart on Chemin de Beau-Rivage. It is quite close."

"Thank you, Sir. That's what I needed to know."

He hung up the receiver and grinned at Isabella. "Guess what, darling? There's a Catholic church just a few blocks from here. It's called the Sacred Heart and the Mass is in English. Shall we attend tomorrow, and see what we think?"

"Yes. What a splendid idea. When do you think we should plan this, assuming we decide upon this Swiss Cathedral?"

"Well, I think we would have to go back and discuss this with your parents. If it weren't for them, we probably never would have found my father. I would never want to hurt their feelings in any way."

"I think they'll understand very well. But, I agree, we do need to speak with them. In fact, we *should* ring them tonight and tell them what we've learned. You know that they are on pins and needles."

"Absolutely. Do it right now, Isabella. I want them to know our good news."

Isabella placed a call to her parents at *Willow Grove Abbey,* and Nan answered. "Nan, it's Isabella. I need to speak to Mummy or Papa. Are they home?"

"Yes, Miss Isabella. I'll get your Mum."

After a moment, Sophia answered the telephone. "Sweetheart, is that you?" she asked.

"Yes, it's me, and Kippy. We've got great news. We found Dieter, and yes, he's definitely Kippy's father. He had facts that prove it beyond any shadow of a doubt. Edwina lied about everything. She had to have known that Dieter was the father. She just wanted to try to get your father to adopt Kippy, thinking he was his biological son. It's all quite unbelievable."

"Oh, my goodness. It's what I suspected. How ghastly of her. I wonder what my father would have thought if he had known that?"

"I imagine he might never have married her. Gosh, it's amazing what lies can do, isn't it?"

"Yes, dear, it is. When are you coming home?"

"Probably the day after tomorrow. I'll let you know for certain. Our one bit of bad news is that Dieter, Kippy's father, is ill. Ironically, he has lung cancer. I think he has some time left, but we're thinking of marrying here in Switzerland, so that he can come to the wedding without a lot of kerfuffle."

"You don't mean now, while you're there?"

"Oh no, Mummy. I could never be married without you with me. We'll come back to England and plan everything. It would probably be quite soon. Then, we'll come back to Switzerland for the ceremony."

"If that's what you want, darling, of course we agree. But, what of all of your English friends?"

"If you like, you could plan a nice reception at *Willow Grove* when we return."

"What a lovely idea. I like that. What of Kippy's religion?"

"He is going to convert. We discussed that before. He can take instructions back home. Tomorrow we're visiting a Catholic church here. It's a lovely old Cathedral in Lausanne. We'll speak with the priest then, so we can find out more. This hotel is incredible. The family can stay here, and any guests who *do* decide to come."

"It all sounds very exciting. Did you like Dieter? How did Kippy feel about him?"

"Yes, actually I did. A lot. He has apparently changed a lot since you met him years ago. He admits that he was a fool about Hitler and his beliefs. That's why he left Germany and chose to live in Switzerland. He never re-married. He has a lovely home, in the countryside and says he loves the peacefulness and quiet. I couldn't help but feel sorry for him. Edwina broke his heart, I think. And then, to learn that he has a son whom he never had a chance to know. It's all very sad."

"Yes, I'm sure it would be. Well sweetheart, I'm delighted you called. Let us know for certain when you'll return. We'll meet your flight."

They hung up, and the room service waiter knocked on the door. Kippy opened it and a large cart covered with warm dishes was rolled in. Kippy had also ordered the best Champagne on the menu. Each of them ordered Beef Wellington, with all of the accompanying dishes and chocolate mousse for dessert. Kippy tipped the waiter and took the lids off the dishes. Then he poured the Champagne and pulled out Isabella's chair.

"I feel like a Princess," she said.

He leaned down and kissed her neck. "You *are* a Princess to me."

"Oh, Kippy. I love you so much. Only one thing that is bothering me."

"What, Honey?"

"I won't have to be Mrs. Kippy Schoen, will I?"

Kippy broke up laughing. "No, but I did figure we'd name our first son Dieter. Don't you think Dieter Crawford would make a nice name?" They both bent over with laughter.

"Hey, beautiful girl, after that sumptuous dinner, I don't know about you, but I could use a nice walk and some fresh air."

"You're on," Isabella answered.

It was a beautiful, June night, and the sky was so clear that the stars looked like diamonds sparkling on the water of Lake Geneva. The air smelled fresh and clean, and there were masses of flowers planted in the design of a large clock on the hotel's front lawn, in front of the terraces.

"I can see why your father chose to live here. It's enchanting."

"Yeah, it really is. I love the cobblestone streets and the architecture."

"It's all so quaint."

"Switzerland had the good sense to stay out of the war. I like their philosophy of neutrality."

"That's probably one reason it's so pristine. They've never suffered the damages of war."

"This has to be a terribly expensive country to live in. Everything seems so clean and neat. It doesn't look like there is any poverty."

"I do think it's expensive. I wonder how your father has been able to afford it for so long. His home is magnificent. He never said what his occupation was. But, he sure didn't make a fortune in the military or in the diplomatic core."

"When I ring him tomorrow, I'll ask. Do you think that would sound rude?"

"No. Of course not. He *is* your father, after all. If he weren't, that would be another thing."

They sat down on a small, marble bench near the shoreline, and Kippy kissed her.

"Do we keep waiting for marriage, Kippy Schoen?" She laughed.

Well. Frau Schoen-to-be, I'd very much like to say 'no more waiting', but we've come this far. A little more time won't kill us. He kissed her again. Um. Imagine what our wedding night will be like."

"I am. I have a feeling we won't get much sleep that night. Speaking of wedding nights, do you have any thoughts about that? A wedding trip? We probably should plan on staying here the first night and then head off on a wedding trip the next day," Isabella suggested.

"Hey. That's my department. I'll make the plans for a wedding trip. I promise I won't disappoint you."

"You could never disappoint me, Kippy. I love you so much." They embraced again.

"Really, Kippy, I'm glad we're going to be able to be honest with our children someday. Won't it be nice to be able to tell them that we treated marriage as the covenant that it is? That what we felt for one another was much more than mere chemistry and that we truly believed each of us was the one God chose for the other?"

"Yes. It will be. The world has changed so much. It seems like in the blink of an eye, everyone is living with someone else and having babies before they've even thought of marriage. They aren't even ashamed of their behavior. Call me old-fashioned, but I'm glad that you chose to do it the right way."

"I didn't choose to do it the right way. The choice was made by God, and I chose to follow his teachings. It really makes life so much simpler, Kippy."

I understand that now, sweetheart. I'm happy that I'm converting and I'm looking forward to it."

"That's the way Mummy said she felt when she converted to marry Papa. Mummy feels that their strong faith is what has kept them together through all of the stress."

"I don't think there's any question that a deep faith gets people through a lot of heartache in life. I hope we don't have to face any heartache, Isabella. We already have had enough anxiety. But, if we do, we will have each other and God will have a prominent place in our lives."

They got up and wandered back to the hotel. It was lit up like a glorious palace and their hearts were filled with happiness.

Chapter Twelve

June 14, 1965

"We've settled on August 15," Isabella announced over breakfast in the dining room at *Willow Grove Abbey*. She and Kippy were eating an early breakfast with her parents. "Kippy will be returning to the States to talk to the CEO at Kaplan about a transfer to their London office. He'll also be asking for a leave of absence for a month, beginning the second week in August. I've already written to Tate Motif's to tell them I'm not returning."

"How do you feel about that, sweetheart?" Spence asked his daughter.

"Oh. A little sad, but there's no contest between leaving Tate's and leaving Kippy. I can't have both. Tate's doesn't have an office in England. I've thought about going into business for myself at some time in the future. I really loved what Kippy and I did with the *Queen Anne*. It would be fun to be involved in another project like that."

"And you two have definitely decided upon being married in Lausanne?" Sophia asked.

"Yes. Absolutely. We visited the Cathedral there and really loved it. It's quite large, and very old. We spoke to the priest after Mass and he was most welcoming. Kippy will be taking instructions at St. Patrick's in New York."

"What about the size of the wedding? Small? Medium? Large?" Sophia inquired.

"Probably small. I don't have many friends who will be able to come over from New York. I can think of three who might, and they would all be my bridesmaids. I have lots of friends from *Ashwick Park* who would probably like to come, but that will depend upon their finances."

"What about you, Kippy?" asked Spence.

My situation would be the same as Isabella's. I have some pretty close friends from Cornell. Also a lot of co-workers from Kaplan, but it's a bit much to ask someone to fly to Switzerland. And, it's not just airfare. The hotels cost a fortune too."

"Well. I have some pretty big news to share with you," began Spence. "I spoke with Dieter this morning on the telephone and he's just a fine chap. I can't believe he's the same man your mother told me about, when he visited here back before the war. I guess people really do grow up. At any rate, we got on extremely well. He's delighted with the fact that Isabella and his son are going to be married. Moreover, he's thrilled that they've decided to do so in Lausanne. Of course, he isn't naïve. He understands precisely why you've chosen to do this. He greatly appreciates it. So much so that he has suggested paying the airline fares and hotel expenses for anyone who would otherwise be unable to attend."

"Oh Papa! How extraordinary! You can't be serious?"

"Yes, indeed I am. I'm going to let him think he's paying for everyone, and then at the end, I'll split the costs with him."

"Can he afford such a thing?" asked Kippy? I forgot to ask him what he did before he became ill. He seems well enough off, but…"

"Kippy. You father is the retired CEO of a major, Pharmaceutical company. Global Pharmaceuticals. I can assure you, he's in good financial shape."

"Well. That's just incredible. I'm so proud of him. It can't have been easy for him to do that, after having been on the Nazi side in the war."

"Apparently, he's exceptionally bright and a hard worker."

"Well, this is a lovely offer for him to make," Isabella interjected.

"You need to make a list and contact the friends you're thinking of inviting. Get in touch with them, so that they know what you're offering. It's a bit improper, but I can't think of any other way. Those who say they would like to attend will be sent a proper invitation. We'll send announcements to the others."

I'm not certain how I shall handle this. I do have some friends who probably *can* afford the trip and accommodations. But, it doesn't seem right to offer the free travel to some and not to others."

Sophia spoke up again. "Darling, tell every one of your friends of Dieter's generosity. I would think those who can afford it, without going into debt, will turn down the offer."

"All right. But, I'll keep the list to a minimum still."

Will you see your father again before the wedding, Kippy?"

"Probably not. But, I'll speak to him on the telephone every night I have a feeling that my arrival in his life has given him new optimism Perhaps it will prove to increase his survival time. I sure hope so."

"We all do, Kippy," Spence answered.

"Mummy,whendoyouwanttogetstartedlookingatweddinggowns? That has to be a number one priority. It will probably take some time, as I'm such a small size that anything I choose will *have* to be special-ordered."

"We'll start at Harrods's tomorrow. I'll need to look at Mother-of-the-Bride dresses too."

"Oh. What fun this is going to be!" Isabella exclaimed. "It's going to be everything I ever dreamed."

"Do you have colors in mind?" Sophia asked.

"Sort-of. I think I want to do something rather different. Such as having each girl wear the same color, but in a different shade, or different but similar dresses. I need to see what the styles look like. I hope I don't have to have something especially designed."

If you decide on the idea of varying shades, what color are you thinking?"

"I think 'yellow,' answered Isabella. "It's a happy, sunny, summer color. You would look gorgeous in it, Mummy. "

"It's always been a favorite of mine."

"Then, yellow it is. I think in varying shades."

I suspect *those will* have to be especially made. But, that's fine. You just need to make decisions about who the girls wearing them will be."

"Mummy. I've thought about asking my cousins. You know, Pippin, Alexandra, Gabriella and Emma. I know I don't know them very well. But, maybe if I asked them, it would put an end to all of this family feuding."

"I think that's a lovely idea, Isabella. I just have no idea what sort of reaction you're likely to get. I don't want you to be hurt. If you decide to ask them, just be prepared for a disappointing response."

"I know. I'll think about it."

"Gosh. It seems like there is so much to do. I never really thought about it. How did you ever get married in such a short time, Mummy?"

Sophia laughed. "Well, when a girl was marrying an RAF pilot who was home on furlough for four days, you just *did* it. Of course, I wore a suit, cut down to fit me, and only had one attendant. Your wedding will be a lot different dear."

"Yes, it will," said Spence. But, you know, I wouldn't change a thing about the way your Mummy and I were married. And look how well it's worked. I guess that's proof that the type of wedding isn't what makes the marriage."

"Does this make me look like a little girl dressed up in her mother's clothing?" Isabella asked her mother, as she came out of the dressing room. It was the tenth gown she had tried that day."

"Well. I *do* have to say it has that look. It's because it's too large, darling."

"The gown can be altered, Miss," the sales lady commented.

"Yes, I know, but I'm not certain it's the proper style for me."

"Perhaps we need to visit the couture houses," her mother suggested.

"Yes. I think so. There are several here now, since the war."

They left Harrods's, and strolled Bond Street, where they found themselves at the Yves St Laurent boutique. As various dresses were brought out for Isabella to see and to try on, they were also plied with fancy chocolates and fine champagne. When the attentive sales associate brought out the next gown, Isabella announced that she had found her wedding dress! It was a dazzling creation designed for a fairytale bride, made of silk taffeta and Battenberg lace, with a very full skirt, short sleeves and a high neckline. In addition the entire dress was trimmed with silk ribbons, woven through the lace to add to the gown's femininity. Roses made of Valenciennes lace draped down the skirt on one side. It was perfect in every way. She would wear flowers and ribbons around a tiara, which would hold a sheer veil. Sophia immediately fell in love with the timeless design. They ordered the dress in a size six, and then moved on to 'Mother of the Bride' dresses.

Isabella had definitely settled on the idea she'd initially broached regarding having the bridesmaids dressed in varying shades of yellow. The hues of yellow would range from Butter-Crème to Lemon, Daffodil, Canary and Buttercup. They would be carrying armloads of fresh jonquils, white peonies and yellow roses. Isabella's bouquet would be a nosegay of yellow and white roses, mixed with lily of the valley and orchids. She gave each bridesmaid was a pair of canary yellow diamond drop earrings. The dresses were already ordered, custom designed by an up and coming husband and wife team in London. Each was the same as the other, but for the variance in color, and was constructed of silk and chiffon, with capped sleeve and round neckline, which dipped into a "V" in the back. The skirt, which was quite full, gathered at the waist and fell softly into yards and yards of fabric.

Isabella had followed Sophia's suggestion and called her cousins to see if they might like to participate in the wedding. Blake's girls, of whom there were three by Susan, and one, Pippin, by his first wife, were all of an age to have made perfect bridesmaids. Unfortunately, when she rang them, each gave one excuse and then another for why they would not be able to take part. Isabella had thought that the generosity of her father and Dieter in paying for airfare and hotel expenses would make the trip a more alluring prospect. On top of that, the Stanton's were paying for the bridesmaid's dresses too. Nevertheless, each one declined the invitation, which clearly meant that Sophia's brothers wouldn't be coming either. It didn't surprise Sophia. She'd more or less expected it, but she felt badly for Isabella. It was sad that on her daughter's wedding day, there would be no family present, other than her parents and her future husband's father. But, Isabella simply said that it was her cousins who would be missing out on a wonderful, lovely occasion. She'd immediately contacted Holly Parsons and Alexandra Stewart, her close friends from *Tunbridge Wells*, and *Ashwick Park*, and also her *Ashwick Park* roommate, Ruth Riverton. Ruth was now an intern at a London hospital. She had followed her dream to become a doctor. Her dearest friends in New York were Francine Rand, and Ruth Beth Branson and they were thrilled to be invited. That gave her a total of five bridesmaids. She chose Holly to be her Maid of Honor, as they had been close friends for such a long time.

Isabella had in mind for her mother a dress of a different style from the maids, in a fabric of crème colored silk with some sort of yellow print. Of course, she knew it would have to be especially made. They were very fortunate, for in looking at fabric swatches, they found a magnificent hand screened silk of crème, with daffodils scattered across the material. Sophia was trying dresses of various designs to see what style she would prefer for the lovely fabric. She went into a fitting room to be measured, while Isabella continued to look about the shop. She picked up a sweet picture hat, swathed with rose point lace and decided to show it to her mother. But, she suddenly came to an abrupt halt as she saw her mother's reflection in the mirror. Sophia was still dressed in a silk slip, bra and panties, but Isabella could clearly see an ugly red scar on her right side, where once her breast had been. The look on Sophia's face changed quickly and she made as if to try to cover herself with a piece of the fabric she was holding in her hand. She acted as if nothing were amiss and continued chatting on about what a lovely bride Isabella was going to be.

Isabella finally found her voice. "Mummy, you needn't pretend with me. I can clearly see that you've had surgery. When did this happen and why?"

"Oh Isabella, it happened last spring. I didn't want to tell you then. You were so busy with your hotel opening and there just never seemed a good time. I went in and had the lump biopsied. It was cancer."

Isabella began to weep. "Oh, no. I couldn't stand it if I lost you, Mummy," she cried.

"Now, there is no reason to think that you're going to lose me. The good news is that it hasn't spread to any other organs or to my lymph nodes. I had the mastectomy and I have followed up with radiation treatment. Of course, they don't consider a person cured unless they have been cancer-free for five years, but I'm feeling fine and have regular exams. You know your father." She laughed.

"Are you sure, Mummy?"

"Absolutely."

"Do you want me to tell Kippy about this, or not?"

"Whatever you wish, Isabella. I think if it were me, I'd want Spence to know. Don't start your marriage with secrets, no matter what they're about."

"I agree, Mummy. He'll be upset, but he'll understand. I wish you had told me. I would have been here."

Sophia put her arms around Isabella. "Sweetheart, your father was with me every moment . Even in the operating room. I had the best care. I didn't want to put a shadow over your wonderful opening of the *Queen Anne*. Now, this is your special time. There is nothing to be worried about and I so want to enjoy every minute of your happiness. So, please dry your tears."

"I'll be all right, Mummy. If you're telling me the truth."

"I've told you exactly what the doctors have told me. Ask Papa. He's been to every appointment I've had."

"That doesn't surprise me. I hope Kippy is as loving and attentive to me as Papa has always been with you."

"Isabella, Kippy loves you very, very much. It's obvious. I think you're getting a fine young man. I think he's the one God wanted you to be with. I really do."

"If I can be half as happy as you and Papa have been, I'd sign on for that tomorrow."

"You will be sweetheart. Probably happier. You've had a much more grounded upbringing. A much, much healthier environment. I think you'll be a wonderful wife."

"I'm so happy, Mummy. Did you feel like this when you married Papa?"

"Oh, yes indeed. I was overjoyed. We'd waited so long. Of course, it was rather spur-of-the moment, but that didn't matter. All that mattered was that we loved each other and wanted to be married before he had to leave to go back to his RAF base. In those days, we never knew when he would be home again. It was ghastly."

"Mummy. Does the fact that you've had breast cancer put me at higher risk for it too?"

"Not necessarily, honey. You should definitely check for lumps and have a physical examination once a year. But, don't get obsessed about it."

"Do you feel all right?"

"Yes. Truly. I feel fine. Now, let's not talk about it anymore for now."

They continued on to the florist who would be doing the flowers for the wedding and spent over two hours explaining exactly what Isabella had in mind. There didn't appear to be a problem with getting the flowers she wanted, as the wedding was in the summer. Not only did they have to discuss bouquets for the bride and bridesmaids, there would be boutonnières for the groomsmen, ushers, groom and both fathers. Then there were the masses of flowers for the church, as well as for the reception. It had been a long day and they still had the drive back to *Willow Grove Abbey*. There were so many things to accomplish before the big day, but the major tasks were underway. The reception was to be held at the Beau-Rivage, where the bridal party and guests would be staying. Sophia and Isabella had spoken with the caterers by telephone and had been posted a long list of delicacies from which to select a menu. The wedding itself was to be at two o'clock in the afternoon, and would then be followed by a splendid wedding reception. There would be tables for the guests, and an orchestra for dancing. They had visited the stationery shop, where they ordered two hundred heavy crème-colored invitations, engraved with the date. August 15. There was a separate card for the reception. Neither Isabella nor Sophia thought two hundred guests would be present, because the wedding was being held in Lausanne, but there were still many people who had shown interest in attending. Even Kippy's old schoolmates from Cornell and Groton, as well as Isabella's friends from Rhode Island School of Design and New York City, not to mention *Ashwick Park School*. It was truly going to be the happiest day in Isabella's life.

Kippy was beside himself with joy. Everything had turned out so well, after all. The only heartache he suffered was the fact that his father was sick. It seemed so unfair that they had only just found each other and now would probably not have many years to really know and love one another as a father and son.

Chapter Thirteen

AUGUST 15, 1965

Isabella stood at the front of the church, next to her father, waiting for the music to begin. She reached over, and kissed Spence lightly on the cheek whispering, "You were my first love," to him. He smiled at her, and touched her cheek. "I've always dreamed of this day, my lovely Isabella. I've watched you grow from a young girl into a stunningly beautiful woman. But, most importantly, I see the same goodness in you that I saw in your mother when we met. Kippy is a lucky fellow and you are a spectacular bride." She watched, as her mother was the last to be escorted into the ceremony. She looked breathtaking in the floral print dress that had been designed for her and her skirt swung to and fro as she made her way down the aisle. Her hair had been cut short again and Isabella thought she resembled a young Elizabeth Taylor. The organ music began and next came the bridesmaids wearing their varying shades of yellow. The daffodils, peonies and roses they carried made them look like springtime maidens about to dance the maypole. Each wore lovely satin slippers on their feet, in a shade of pale yellow. The earrings Isabella had presented to each of them were gleaming at their ears and necks, creating tiny flashes of glitter. Isabella took her father's arm. She'd thought she would be nervous but she wasn't. Ahead at the altar, she could see her wonderful Kippy, standing next to his best man. He looked so handsome, with his bright blonde hair shining in the sunlight streaming through the stained glass windows. Everything was perfect. There were masses of roses at the altar and ribbons adorned each pew. Her gown fit to perfection and in her hands was the nosegay of yellow and white roses, mixed with lily of the valley, and orchids. Kippy had given Isabella pearl and diamond earrings and she wore the pearls her mother had worn when she married Spence. She felt as though she were in a fairytale.

Dieter was sitting in the front row, on the groom's side, looking terribly proud. Isabella felt dreadful that he didn't have any other family to share in his happiness. But then, as she entered the sanctuary, she noticed that the sweet housekeeper, whom she and Kippy had met when they first visited Dieter, was sitting next to him. So, he wasn't alone after all. She glanced to the left, and saw her mother, looking young enough to be the bride. She was still so beautiful. The yellow hue of her splendid dress showed off her dark hair and olive coloring. She wore a pillbox hat on her head, with yellow flowers surrounding it. Isabella caught her eye and Sophia blew her a silent kiss. When they reached the altar, the priest asked, "Who gives this young lady to be married to this man?" Spence replied "Her mother and I do," placing her hand in Kippy's. They both looked into each other's eyes with deep love and Isabella smiled a lovely smile. Then Spence took his seat next to Sophia. There were tears in both of their eyes. The Catholic ceremony was longer than most of the guests, who were protestant, were used to. But, it was such a beautiful setting, that no one got tired of the ritual. When they repeated the marriage vows, Isabella spoke in a strong, determined voice, and Kippy did as well. Then there was the exchanging of the rings, a final prayer during which they knelt at the altar, and finally the kiss everyone was waiting for. As they moved out of the cathedral, arm in arm, they both had tears of joy, and wonderful smiles on their faces.

It was a perfectly splendid day. The sky was as blue as the water in Lake Geneva and the temperature was in the mid-seventies. The photographer took several pictures of the couple, and the bridal party in front of the lovely, old cathedral. Then, when they returned to the *Beau- Rivage* for the reception, there were more photos taken on the lovely flower filled lawn that sloped to the water. When they entered the ballroom at the hotel, Isabella gasped. It was all so incredibly beautiful. Masses and masses of yellow daffodils, white lilies, yellow roses, orchids and purple iris, mixed with blue hyacinth and white hydrangeas adorned the ballroom. They were banked where Isabella and her mother would receive. In addition, they spilled from a quaint and charming arbor, where Isabella and Kippy would stand for photos with each of their special wedding participants. Just as at Sophia's debut ball, there were silver urns spilling forth flowers on every flat surface. The fragrance in the room was delightful. It was such fun to see all of their friends from New York City, and from the years preceding when they both were in school. Everyone wished that they had more time to really visit, and chat about what had happened in each of their lives, but a wedding was a wedding, not a reunion. Still, they did spend a lot of time with dear, old friends. They ate a scrumptious meal, followed by several hours of dancing. The music was a mixture of 1960's modern, and melancholy songs of the war years. Everyone stood back and watched when Sophia, Spence, Isabella and Kippy took to the floor. What a lovely sight they were. Isabella had never dreamed that so many people would attend. Nearly all of the two hundred invitations had been accepted and not even half had made use of the generous offer for airfare and hotel accommodations.

Finally, it was time for Isabella to change into her going away outfit so she and her mother disappeared up to their suite. Isabella had selected a simple, elegant, white silk dress, with long sleeves, and a high neck. She brushed her hair out, and let it fall to her shoulders, in a fresh, natural look. She and Kippy paused at the top of the stairway and Isabella tossed her bridal bouquet. Ruth Riverton caught it. Her date was a handsome young intern at the hospital where she was assigned and everyone began to tease him about being next. The bride and groom ran through a shower of rose petals from the doorway of the *Beau-Rivage*, and Isabella was astounded to see a horse drawn carriage waiting for them. Kippy had arranged this surprise. She was laughing and crying as she crawled up onto the seat of the carriage and they both waved until they could no longer see anyone. Isabella had no idea where they were going. The only thing she had asked was that it be someplace warm. The first night would be spent in Lausanne and then they would depart for their honeymoon.

The carriage delivered them to the Lausanne Palace and Spa, built in 1915, and one of the most elegant hotels in Europe. Kippy had reserved the bridal suite on the top floor, which afforded breathtaking views of Lake Geneva. Their luggage had been sent ahead, so they didn't have to worry about that, as they disembarked and entered the grand palace. Kippy registered at the front desk and a bellman took them up to their suite, which was pure, unadulterated luxury. Kippy put his arms around her, and kissed her longingly. "No more waiting, Mrs. Crawford," he laughed.

"And I'm so terribly glad, my wonderful husband," she smiled.

He opened the bottle of champagne on the tea table, and poured each of them a flute. They toasted one another over and over, until the bottle was nearly empty. Then, Isabella announced that she was going to change into something comfortable, and disappeared into the bath. They were both giggling by that time.

How times had changed since Sophia's day. When she had married Owen Winnsborough, she'd taken fourteen peignoirs on her wedding trip. Isabella had a few, darling silk teddies for nightwear. But, her favorite piece of all was a Pucci short gown, sleeveless, and V-necked, with a matching short robe. The colors were typically Pucci. Wild lavenders and blues swirled together with pink. This was her choice for the wedding night. She was so tiny and her legs were lovely, so the entire effect was adorable. She bathed, brushed her hair, bushed her teeth, and added perfume. She had no need for make-up, but for a bit of lip gloss, and a hint of pink blush. She left her hair in the cascading curls that she knew Kippy liked.

When she emerged from the bath, Kippy was talking on the telephone in the parlor. He was speaking with his father, thanking him for all he had done to make their day so special. Apparently, he had already telephoned Sophia and Spence, thanking them as well. She was overwhelmed with pride at that fact that he had taken the time to be thoughtful to both his family and hers. He, too, had changed clothing and was dressed in a pair of crisp, white Brooks Brother's pajamas, with a monogram on the cuff sleeve. He stood when she entered the room, and came to her.

"You were the most beautiful bride in the world today, darling. I was very, very proud of you and I am now so honored to be able to say that you're my wife. I'll never tire of using that word. I love you so much, Isabella." He took her in her into his arms and embraced her closely. She put her arms around his neck, and kissed him back, with all of the love she had to give.

"I feel like the luckiest girl on Earth, Kippy. Thank God we found each other."

"I agree with your parents. I think that was bound to happen, no matter where we'd been." They kissed again, with heightened passion. Then, he took her by the hand, and led her into the lovely bedroom. The bed had been turned down, and there were yellow, crisp bed linens. Kippy had asked the maids to scatter rose petals on the sheets. In addition, an enormous bouquet of roses sat on the end table, next to a second bottle of champagne. "Was this your idea?" She murmured, as she kissed him again.

"It seemed a nice finishing touch to a perfect day," he replied.

"I adore you, my wonderful husband. Absolutely adore you."

He reached and touched her porcelain cheeks, and then ran both hands through her long hair. "I've wanted to do that all day."

She reached up and put both of her hands in his hair, "So have ," she smiled.

They tumbled backwards onto the soft bed, and continued kissing. It felt so wonderful to know that this time she didn't have to say 'no'. Kippy was determined to go very slowly, as he didn't want to frighten her. The last thing he wanted was to hurt her. He began to kiss her neck, and then proceeded downward to her breasts. Slowly he slipped the Pucci gown over her head. She wasn't the least embarrassed. Her body was remarkable. The skin on her legs and breasts felt like silk. He ran his hand up her thigh and she reached up and unbuttoned his pajama top. Soon they were lying together naked. She had never before felt such a sensation. All the while he continued to kiss her, and murmur sweet words in her ear. She ran her hand down his chest, and felt the hair grow thicker as she reached lower and lower. Kippy was surprised at her boldness, for a girl who'd had no experience before. He placed his hand between her legs, and felt that she was moist and warm. "Oh Kippy, I never dreamed I could feel this way," she whispered. "You're so beautiful, Isabella. So beautiful. "Kippy sighed. He put two fingers inside that warm, petal-like opening and she began to moan softly. She burrowed into him, to be as close as she could. "Oh Kippy. I want you so." Slowly and gently, he lowered himself upon her. She gasped when he entered her, but only for a moment. Her hips raised up to meet his, and he began to thrust, very carefully and very slowly. He could feel her welcoming him into her body with each thrust. Suddenly, he could feel that he had broken the barrier, where no other man had been before.

Isabella grew warm all over and she felt as if she were floating. Up, up, up. She was climbing to a place she'd only heard of, which no words could describe. She called out his name as she reached that pinnacle of passion, and gripped him tightly. *Bliss.* That was the only word she could think of that could possibly describe her emotions. *Pure bliss.* Kippy cried out her name, as he collapsed on top of her and lay on her breast breathing heavily. "My God, Isabella. I was expecting quite a tepid experience for your first time, but that was sensational. I didn't hurt you, did I?"

"Not a bit, darling. What an incredible feeling. I felt like we just melted together as one person."

"That's the way it's supposed to be, precious. I promise you, it will get even better. I tried to be very careful."

"If it gets much better, I don't think I can stand it," she gently laughed.

He continued to run his fingers through her gorgeous hair and she played with a lock of his. They lay together, quietly savoring the aftermath of their love. Then, Kippy reached over and picked up the bottle of champagne from the bed's side table. He tipped it on its side and let a bit of it run onto her breasts. Then, he put his mouth on her, and tasted the sweetness of the wine. He could tell she was becoming aroused again. He poured some more of the champagne a little lower down, and once again drank of her beauty. He pulled her closer to him, and entered her with tenderness. They both called out to one another in a duet of love. They finally fell asleep as the sun was rising, wrapped in one another's arms.

They woke, still in each other's arms, and made love again. Isabella wondered if she could ever get enough of him. Finally, they left the bed, and went into the bath, where they showered together. Isabella shocked herself, because only a day ago she couldn't have imagined such a thing. Now, it seemed that nothing was out of bounds. He soaped her back and she soaped his. She could see that he wanted her once again. She had so much to learn, but was so glad that she had waited until she had Kippy to teach her. Acts which would once have seemed terribly inappropriate had become merely ways to love one another and show pleasure.

They finally toweled off, and began to dress. Isabella twisted her long hair into a knot on top of her head, and put on a casual summer dress. She had asked Kippy where they were going, but all he would say was that she would not need any warm clothes. It was to be a surprise. She laughed and said "I'm glad you said 'warm' clothes. I was afraid there for a moment that you were going to say that I didn't need *any* clothes, and then I would have worried that you'd scheduled us for a nudist camp!"

"No. Nothing so risqué. However, now that you mention it, that wouldn't have been such a bad idea. But, I don't want any other men looking at you."

"No worry, darling. None ever has and none ever will."

He gave her a sweet kiss.

They checked out of the hotel and got into their rental car. She could tel from the map on the front seat that they were driving south but that could have meant anything. After over two hours of driving, over the Alps, they stopped for lunch at a small roadside Inn. They were still in Switzerland. but on the border of Italy. She would like to have been visiting Italy, as she loved it so, but she rather hoped that they could save that trip for another time. She wanted nothing to remind her of any other time in her life, and Italy, of course, reminded her of Lucca. She had, in fact, invited Lucca to the wedding, and felt nothing but friendliness for him. But she wanted the memories of her wedding trip to be of someplace she had never been before. Finally, over lunch, Kippy told her that they were headed to Portofino, a breathtaking port on the Italian Riviera. Back in the car, they drove to Santa Margherita, another lovely village, where frequent ferries ran to Portofino. Portofino is a car-free town, so they left theirs in a secure space, designed for such a purpose, and boarded the next ferry that came along.

Portofino was not a well-known place at that time. Occasionally one heard of a movie star visiting there. After about a half hour ride, the picturesque village came into view. It was a half-moon shaped, seaside village with pastel houses lining the shore of the harbor. Isabella was entranced. It was a fairytale setting, with its crystalline aquamarine waters, and a castle atop a hill. They could see their hotel, The Splendido, sitting high above the harbor, which had once been an ancient monastery. When they disembarked at the dock, a representative from the hotel met them, and loaded their luggage onto a motorized cart. Then, he told them to sit in the front with him and they made their way up the steep, winding path to the grand hotel. The higher they climbed, the more awe-inspiring the view. Both Kippy and Isabella were overwhelmed at the sensational beauty surrounding them. When they arrived in front of the hotel, they disengaged from the cart and the gentleman who had met them followed with their luggage. Their bedroom was elegantly furnished, with an ocean view balcony overlooking an infinity pool, and four acres of tropical gardens. There was no question that it inspired pure romance and Isabella wasn't surprised to learn that this was where Richard Burton had proposed to Elizabeth Taylor in 1964. She walked out to the balcony.

"Oh, Kippy. This is just so incredible. Warm sun, beautiful water, and a sea breeze. What more could a person ask for? I'm so glad you chose such a stunning spot. It's just perfect."

"I agree. I didn't want to spend our wedding trip at someplace banal or run-of-the-mill, and this certainly isn't," he laughed, kissing her on the neck. "It appears to be everything I was told it would be."

"Do you know someone who has been here?"

"Yes. A fellow in my office took a cruise that made a call here. He didn't stay at this hotel, but he walked up the path to see it. He told me he'd vowed to book a room here, if he ever returned."

Isabella turned and walked back into the suite. It was decorated in soft shades of white, pale greens, and taupe. She unpacked her luggage, hanging everything in the large closet. Kippy did the same. When they were finished, they decided to meander down to the poolside restaurant, and have a drink. They felt like they were in paradise. Just as they were about to leave the room, the telephone rang. It surprised both of them for they couldn't imagine who would be ringing. Perhaps it was just the front desk.

"This is Mr. Crawford," Kippy said.

"Mr. Crawford, I have a long distance call for you from England. Will you please hold while I notify the operator that I have you on the line?"

"Yes, of course," Kippy answered.

There was some crackling noise and then silence, and finally Spence's voice could be heard.

"Kippy? This is Spence Stanton. Can you hear me?"

"Yes. Just fine. We didn't expect to hear from you. This is a nice surprise."

"Are you both well? I hope I didn't interrupt anything. I'm glad that I caught you in."

"Yes. We're both fine. Very happy. This place is really something. We just got in a bit ago. Is everything all right at home?"

"Everything is all right with Sophia and me, but there *is* a problem. I'm sorry to have to interrupt your wedding trip, but Sophia thought I should contact you."

"No. That's fine, Spence. What's the problem? Nothing serious, I hope?"

"Well. Yes, it *is* quite serious. Let me start at the beginning. While we were all gone, but for the servants, your Uncle Eugene seems to have had another of his foolish ideas."

"Oh no. What's he done now? I really thought I took care of him when I saw him the last time."

"Apparently, he planned to burn *Willow Grove Abbey* to the ground. The fool. He sneaked over here in the dead of night and poured kerosene all around the base of the house, along the back. Then he set it afire. Of course, it all went up in a tremendous blaze."

"You mean the house went up in a blaze?"

"No. The Kerosene. The dogs began to bark, and that woke Nan who ran down the stairway, and out the back kitchen door. She saw the flames and ran back to get a bucket of water. Eugene saw her and grabbed hold, trying to keep her from ruining his plans. By that time she had a bucket in her hands. She poured water on some of the fire, and then she hit Gene in the head with the bucket, since he kept pulling on her, to keep her away. He went down into the flames. Nan tried her best to get him out of there, but she couldn't do it. His shirt had caught fire. Nan ran into the house and rang the fire lads. Then, she brought more water out and tried again to staunch the flames on her own. Of course it was no use. She then tried to drag Eugene out of the burning flames, but she isn't anywhere near strong enough to accomplish such a feat. All she could do was wait for the fire chaps. They arrived and quickly got the fire under control. They took Eugene to the hospital. He was dead on arrival, Kippy. I'm sorry. It was smoke inhalation, so I don't believe he suffered greatly."

"What about *Willow Grove Abbey*?"

"Extensive damage to the rear of the house. But, insurance will take care of that. We thought you should know about your uncle. Nan feels dreadful, of course."

"Nan shouldn't feel dreadful at all. It wasn't her fault. If he hadn't tried something so idiotic, it wouldn't have happened. I'm glad she wasn't harmed. Of course, I'm sorry about him, Spence, but anyone who would do something so dimwitted has to have been mentally unbalanced. If it weren't for Nan's good thinking, we might have lost the entire house. I can't imagine what Gene hoped to accomplish by something so evil."

"I suppose it was his way of getting back at you, for not going along with his plans."

"Well, I'll call my Aunt Fiona, who is probably the sanest one of them all and she can take care of it. He's done his last damage to me, and to your family, thank God. Isabella and I will come back home as soon as possible."

"Oh Kippy, I hate for you to do that. There is really nothing that you can accomplish here. I've got a crew coming to temporarily seal off the damaged area. We won't be able to start any re-building until the insurance fellows come around."

"All right, Spence. Isabella and I will stay here a few days then. I'll ring and let you know our plans before we leave. Thanks a lot for calling. I'm sorry."

"Nothing for you to be sorry about. Kiss Isabella and we'll speak later. Goodbye."

Kippy hung up the telephone and put his head in his hands. "Good God, Isabella, that damned uncle of mine tried to burn down *Willow Grove Abbey*. All he succeeded in was causing some damage to the house, and killing himself in the process."

"Gene is dead? My God. Tell me what happened," she answered.

Kippy repeated his conversation with Spence.

"Kippy, your uncle must have been totally daft. Thank God he cidn't accomplish what he set out to do. I'm sorry that he died. I know you must feel some sadness. After all, he was your uncle. But, Kippy, I just can't imagine such a thing."

He went to Isabella and held her in his arms. "You know, sweetheart, I suppose I should feel some kind of sorrow, but I have to admit that I don't. Gene just wasn't a very good person and that is putting it mildly. He was obsessed. Honestly, I just feel relieved that he won't be causing any more trouble. Do you think that's awful of me?"

"No, darling, of course not. He caused you a lot of pain, and me too, for that matter. What did Papa say about the house? It won't have to be torn down, will it?"

"No. Nothing as drastic as that. There was mostly damage to the back side. Are you all right, Isabella? Do you want to go back to England right away?"

"Not unless you think we should."

"No. Your father didn't feel that there was anything we could do. Let's go on with our plans, and stay for the week. If we change our minds, we can always alter our plans."

They kissed one another and Isabella buried her head on Kippy's chest. "I think we need that drink more than ever," she smiled up at him.

Chapter Fourteen

August 23, 1965

$\mathcal{I}$t was a week that neither Kippy nor Isabella would ever forget. They managed not to let their bad news from England ruin such a glorious time and enjoyed their heavenly surroundings. They felt such enormous delight in their love, and in the newness of marriage. One night they would eat a casual dinner on the terrace, and another in the more formal, elegant dining room in the hotel. The hand painted walls, in cool watercolors, and the black and white marble floors created a stylish backdrop for a refreshing aperitif in the cocktail bar, or an after-dinner drink serenaded by rich piano music. They took a sunset cruise one night, where they enjoyed cocktails and canapés, while watching the sun go down. On another day they visited the incomparable Cinque Terre; five picturesque villages; Monterosso, Vernazza, Corniglia, Manarola and Riomaggiore, linked by a coastal path that wound through vineyards, whites and beaches, and rocky seascapes. Another day they tried their hand at deep sea fishing, with their own private guide. At the end of each day, they returned to their lovely room, and fell into one another's arms. It all seemed to end much too soon. They vowed to return to that magnificent hotel, overlooking the Ligurian Sea, every year on their anniversary.

When their airplane landed at Heathrow, Sophia and Spence were there to meet them. Kippy and Isabella looked refreshed from the sun and the sea, and a bit frazzled from too many late nights drinking Galliano on the rocks, and making love until dawn. It was wonderful to see Spence and Sophia waiting at the arrivals gate as they completed their trek through customs. There were big hugs, and kisses all around, and then they quickly moved to the baggage area where they retrieved their luggage. When they were finally in the car, and headed to *Willow Grove Abbey*, the conversation was taken up with Eugene's dreadful attack on their home, and plans for reconstruction. Spence shocked them when he told them that he thought he had reached a decision which could affect all of them, regarding converting *Willow Grove Abbey* into a Country House Hotel. Isabella was stunned. At first it seemed like a ghastly idea, and she said so. "Papa, you can't be serious. Why would we want to do such a thing? I can't imagine my childhood home becoming a place where strangers can simply come and go at will."

They arrived at the *Abbey* and the chauffeur dropped them at the front entrance. He said that he would make certain their bags were sent directly to their room. Entering the house, Isabella was still in a fright about the thought that *Willow Grove Abbey* might become a tourist lodging. They settled themselves in the drawing room, and Nan brought them hot tea.

"Just listen to me, darling, before you make any quick judgments," Spence implored.

"All right. But, I really don't think you can convince me to be in favor of such a change."

"Isabella, the idea would make a great deal of sense. It's getting more and more expensive for the upkeep on a house this old. It is so massive and there is no way on Earth we need so much room. We don't live the sort of life that was lived in the old days. Very few people can afford such luxury. It takes an enormous staff to keep it top notch at all times. The grounds alone are an enormous cost. Even if money weren't an issue…And it isn't the primary reason your mother and I are considering this. People just don't live this way anymore. It's much too formal and grand. Yet, outsiders are potty about seeing the way people once lived in these old mansions. Many of the old Country houses are now charging for tourists to tramp through and get a gander at the interior of their residences. I don't care for that idea at all. Yet, I do think that such a splendid house, where so many memories have been made, and where so much craftsmanship is apparent, should be seen and admired. *Willow Grove Abbey* was meant to be a family home, where lovely dinners are served, and splendid gatherings take place in the Drawing Room, and even the Ballroom."

"I love this house more than life itself," said Sophia, "yet I must say that my happiest days were spent in our charming home at *Tunbridge Wells*. We lived so much more simply then."

"Could you explain exactly what you have in mind, Sir?" asked Kippy.

"Have you ever had occasion to stay in an old Country House Hotel in England, Kippy? There are some very charming ones."

"No. I can't say that I have. I do know of some though."

"Yes. Well, our idea would be to convert *Willow Grove* into a warm, welcoming haven for persons who want a get-a-way and who want to live for a few days or weeks as the old families once did. We would want our guests to enter this Palladian mansion and take a step back in time to a by-gone era of opulence and romance. *Willow Grove* would be unique, because it's adorned with original, antique furnishings, sumptuous fabrics, and Waterford crystal chandeliers. Yet a warm welcome and homey atmosphere prevails."

"I'm beginning to have a vision of what it might be like," Isabella joined in. "Kippy, we could do it rather in the same vein that we did the *Queen Anne* in New York. Each room would have its own, special charm. We could use the same theme. Name each room after a famous English author, or a character from a classic book, and then decorate it accordingly. There are so many, many rooms. Twenty-two bedrooms in all, and so many of them have an adjoining parlor. Most have their own baths already, so that wouldn't be a problem. The reception rooms are already beautiful. What a lovely place this would be to bring a family for a special holiday. But, would all of this be manageable? Wouldn't it cost heaps of money to restore everything? And wouldn't we need to hire much more staff? Also, we have the stables. We could add a few horses, so guests could enjoy a ride over the gorgeous countryside."

"Now you're seeing it the way I've pictured it," Spence answered. "Yes, it would indeed cost quite a good bit, but I think within bounds. We would ensure that *Willow Grove Abbey* could continue to be the remarkable home it's always been. I'm quite certain that it could be placed on the Historic Register. Of course, this would be extremely upscale. Very pricey."

"Well, we proved that such a concept could work when we did the *Queen Anne*. It's highly successful, and growing more so every day. We could arrange for the same sort of accoutrements, such as a car and driver to meet guests at the airport or train station, and animal friendly accommodations. Dining would be done family-style, I should think, either in the formal dining room, or in the smaller breakfast room. We would serve afternoon tea in the drawing room," Isabella continued. "Oh, my mind is just whirling with wonderful thoughts and images."

"I had a feeling that once you thought about it, it would intrigue you, Isabella. In fact, you and Kippy are just perfect for this sort of project," Sophia said.

"But, I go back to the money. Have you a figure in mind for all of this luxury?" asked Kippy.

"Not precisely, Kippy. I think you're better at that sort of thing than I am," Spence laughed. "But, remember, we own the house free and clear, since we bought out Sophia's brothers years ago, so we start with the property unencumbered. From there, it's a matter of décor, stables, horses, staff, and so forth. Can you put pen to paper, and come up with a fairly good estimate, Kippy?"

"Yes. Sure. And Isabella will need to do an estimate on what the inside décor would cost."

"Who would be managing it?" Isabella asked.

"You and Kippy," I should think, answered Spence.

Isabella looked at Kippy, and gave him a huge smile. "Oh, Kippy, we could work together on this, and then work side by side in the running of the hotel. We both have perfect training for this. What a remarkable idea."

"That's what Sophia and I thought," Spence answered. You know how I feel about things that are meant to be. I don't believe that it's a coincidence that the two of you have the training and experience that you do, and that you've landed in the perfect spot to put it to use on a grand scale."

"*Serendipity*," Sophia and Isabella said at the same time.

"What's 'serendipity'?" asked Kippy.

"It just means 'fate' or 'destiny,' that something was meant to be. All of my parent's lives that word has been their touchstone. So many things that have happened seemed to be ordained."

"Well, this idea of converting Willow Grove into a spectacular country house hotel does seem to have been predestined. I'm really enthused about it," Kippy answered.

After weeks of planning and late nights sitting up trading ideas with one another, the project was firmly decided. What with Kippy's inheritance from both his adoptive parents and Nigel Somerville, plus Isabella's own inheritance, there didn't appear to be any difficulty with the cost. Spence and Sophia had a very good income from the Winnsborough Clinic, and Spence also received very nice royalties from his books. Spence had a barrister draw up papers, forming a partnership, naming Kippy *Chairman of the Board* and Isabella *President*. Spence and Sophia were also officers, but they wanted the primary responsibility to be Kippy and Isabella's.

The last decision to be made was where everyone would live. They concluded that all of the staff would remain in their current accommodations within the *Abbey*. After a long walk about the property, Kippy and Isabella fell in love with the old caretaker's cottage on the grounds, and the cost of renovating it and making it into a darling home for them was added into the total. Finally, Spence and Sophia announced that they would move into the Dower house near the main entrance to the *Abbey*. It was a charming home, built of stone. It was significantly smaller in size than the *Abbey*, but still very grand. Sophia and Spence could see how, with a bit of change in décor, it could be made into a perfectly delightful spot for them to settle into for the remainder of their lives. Once all of the decisions were made, the work began.

Sophia and Spence were glad to be able to escape to their clinic every morning, as the racket made by the construction lads was enough to drive them mad. They moved to the Dower house at once, so that they would be out of the melee that was occurring in the main house. While they were gone during the day, the Dower house was turned into an enchanting home. It took many months for *Willow Grove Abbey* to begin to live up to the image that the family had envisioned, but when it did, they all agreed that the wait had been worth it. Isabella oversaw the decorating of each

room to perfection, and Kippy interviewed additional staff, so that those
who had been at Willow Grove for a long time could serve as Managers
of those new to the hotel. When the last draperies had been hung, the last
wallpaper put up, and the last fluffy towels hung on the warmers in the
baths they all stood back and marveled at what had been accomplished.

Just as with the *Queen Anne*, the publicity had been massive, and by
the time the opening day was in sight, the hotel was already booked completely through Christmas. 1966. The opening of *Willow Grove Abbey* was
less ostentatious than that of *The Queen Anne*, primarily because of its
Country House atmosphere. Still, a large Ball was scheduled for the first
night. Sophia couldn't help but compare it to her debut ball in that same
room, in 1935. New chandeliers had been hung down the center of the
room, and a bandstand had been built to accommodate musicians at one
end. The lovely, old baby grand piano that had been at the house since
time immemorial, still stood in its place of honor. The beautiful, ancient
wooden floors had been completely restored and had a gorgeous sheen.
Masses of flowers were banked in every corner of the enormous room. The
orchestra played all of the old war years songs, and it truly was like stepping
back into history when one entered the magnificent room. It had been
thirty years since Sophia had twirled around and around in her incredible
white gown, yet it seemed like only yesterday. On the night of the Grand
Opening, Sophia took that same breathtaking dress out of the cedar-lined
closet where it had hung in a protected bag all of those years. It still looked
like it was brand new. She had planned on purchasing something new to
wear to the Grand Opening, but when Spence saw her in that original
dress, the one she had worn the night he fell in love with her, he made her
promise that she would wear it again. It was testament to the way she had
kept her figure that the gown still fit exactly as it had in 1935. Isabella also
wore a white gown, with a high, Victorian collar, and Alencon lace covered
sleeves. It was constructed of white taffeta, with an overlay of exquisite,
hand embroidered chiffon. She wore her hair in an upsweep, and placed
flowers at the crown. Spence, Sophia, Isabella and Kippy met the guests
as they entered the ballroom, welcoming them to *Willow Grove Abbey*.
There were many famous people present, and all were enthralled at what
had been accomplished at that beautiful, four hundred year-old mansion.

The newspapers and several well-known magazines had sent reporters and photographers to cover the story, and many photos would appear in the next day's press.

They danced and danced, and drank far too much champagne. The guests had a marvelous time, and when Spence and Sophia crept away to their lovely, Dower House, they saw a family surrounding the piano in the drawing room, singing "There'll be Bluebirds over the White Cliffs of Dover." The sun was just rising, casting shadows of pink on the terrace, where a young girl and a handsome gentleman could scarcely be seen through the mist of early morning.

Chapter Fifteen

SUMMER, 1968
SOPHIA

*A*nd so it has ended; not as I dreamed it would, but in a rather poignant manner. It is 1968, and I am fifty-one years old this year. Spence will turn 58. We have been married nearly twenty eight years in December, and I still weep when I hear songs from those sad, but romantic war years, which have now become somewhat fascinating to the younger generation. I still remember gliding across posh hotel dance floors, with Spence holding me closely, while I buried my face in his crisp blue, RAF shirt. Some of those very songs are becoming popular once again and I stop and listen when I hear young people blaring them from their automobile radios. Will anyone ever know as romantic a time as we did? I suppose every generation thinks that. But, ours was truly unique. We lived from moment to moment, never knowing what would come next, never knowing whether we would see one another again after we said "goodbye".

Mine has been an extraordinary life. I now believe as Spence always has, that it really *was* all meant to be. Surely, the fact that Kippy and Isabella found one another again, and fell so deeply in love, proves that beyond any shadow of a doubt. They seem to have been meant to be in New York at the same time, and to have employment that offered them an opportunity to meet. The odds of that happening are just too overwhelming. So, just as God led me to my soul mate on a spring night in 1935, He took hold of Isabella's hand and led her to New York City, where on a fine April evening in 1964, she met her soul mate again, even though she had no recollection of having met him before.

For all of the upheaval and trauma, my life has been a good one. I've spent the majority of it with the man I adore and I've been blessed with the most wonderful daughter any mother could ever have wished for. My beloved *Willow Grove Abbey* is safe and secure for at least another generation, and probably beyond that. I love knowing that other families, besides our own, will be able to enjoy my lovely home, and carry their own memories away with them when they leave.

I have sorrow because I never was able to make amends with my brothers, but the truth is that we were never a particularly close family from the beginning, and while that's what I yearned for, it simply wasn't to be. We were such children when it all began, and it took years for all of us to come away from the confusion and chaos that reigned for so long in our home. Perhaps it was too much to expect that three children could grow up in such chaos and tumult, and develop into loving adults. There certainly wasn't much love in our home. I thank God that Isabella has had a much more tranquil upbringing, in spite of the war. I made very foolish choices early in life, and they caused great pain. Again, I credit God with letting me see the wisdom in his commandment "Thou Shalt Not Lie".

When I look back now, I realize that Spence was not only meant to be my loving husband, but also my guide through life. For that's certainly what he has been to me. His sensible, level-headed intelligence helped me through so many parts of my growth. What might have become of me had I not had him by my side? I shudder to think. But, I don't brood over those possibilities, because I *do* firmly believe that any future without Spence in it simply could not have been. God had a plan for us, and wisely, Spence knew which path to follow.

Why have I written it all down? For a variety of reasons, I suppose. It was always in my nature to keep a journal. That began at *Ashwick Park*. I felt terribly alone, so much of the time. Writing down feelings and thoughts, as well as happenings was good for my soul. When the war came, I knew I would want to have a record of each and every moment during that historical era. I wanted to write down how I felt when I had to spend so much time apart from my "dashing RAF pilot." Actually, all of those memories are seared into my soul, and I really don't need a journal or any other written document to help me remember them. But, I wanted Isabella to understand, when she was old enough, everything that happened during those years of her life, and this journal seemed to be the best vehicle. As the years went by, it became a habit, of sorts, and I continued on. I want Isabella to have *my* story, which is also very much *her* story too. I want her to understand how my love for her father was the sort that never stopped growing. I pray that her love for Kippy will be the same. I want her to know how dearly I have loved him, and of course, how much I adored her from the moment I first set eyes upon her. I want her to understand lessons I learned through my own growth, and hope that she will see and understand that taking the right path will always bring you to the place you need to be. Sometimes, God has a strange way of leading us where we need to go. But, in the end, He always does. Not all stories have happy endings.

DECEMBER, 1968
SPENCE

I want to speak about the lady whom I married. She was a lady in every way. The title that she carried as an honorific was the very least of the ways in which she lived up to that word *Lady*. Yes, she was that, but not only because she was the daughter of a titled aristocrat. Early on, when we first met, I wished she hadn't been of that lineage. It would have made our love so much easier. When I saw her for the first time at her début ball, I was utterly speechless. I'd seen many beautiful women by that point in my life, but Sophia's beauty was different from all of the rest. It shone from within. She was so young, and innocent, and though I'm not sure she was aware of it, she was a lost soul. There are so many things I should have done differently. First and foremost, I should never have let her go to see her parents without me by her side, after the weekend we spent in *Twigbury*. She was so honest and I should have known that there was no way she wouldn't tell them that she loved me and wanted their blessing for us to marry. If I had been with her, no matter how violent the meeting had been, there would never have been the need for her to run to Edwina when she learned she was pregnant, or reason to ever have married Owen Winnsborough. We would never have lost those years we were apart. I was wrong to blame her for lying to me. She was such a frightened, little rabbit, and I still can only imagine how terrified she must have been when she learned that she was going to have my child. Thank God she never wavered about whether she wanted to keep the baby or not. If she made mistakes, they were out of fear; fear for me, and fear for her unborn child. I should have seen that.

Even after all of the years we spent together, there are so many things I hope she knew. I once told her, long ago, that I thought the essence of beauty was wit, kindness, intelligence and outer appearance. She had them all. But, to that list I would add, an inner resilience She has had an ability to move on, over and over again, when life dealt harsh blows, and it seemed she'd been defeated. I would also add the ability to give unconditional love, even though the people who hurt her probably didn't deserve it. And, perhaps most of all, I should add that she understood forgiveness, better than anyone I've ever known. I'll always wish that her family might have understood her the way I did. They would have seen a gracious, generous, kind lady, who desperately needed love, and who had an abundance of it to give. Her brothers' lives would have been far richer for having recognized that.

As you have probably gathered, we lost Sophia on December 27, 1968. Incredibly, it was our wedding anniversary. The cancer that had caused such fear in 1965, returned with a vengeance, in March of 1968. By the time we were able to take her to the specialists she needed, it was already too late. True to form, she fought with all of the spirit she'd always shown when up against a foe. But, finally she became tired, and told me that she was glad that she was going to leave this world before me. She admitted that her strongest fear had always been the idea of living without me by her side. Strange, for living without Sophia has always been my greatest fear too.

Now, I spend a lot of time by her grave, where she waits for me to join her, in the ancient burying ground at her beloved *Willow Grove Abbey*. I have planted so many blooms on her grave, that one can scarcely see the etching on her stone. I know she would be happy about that. I try not to be burdensome with my grief. I hold it inside, where it belongs, next to the image of her that I carry in my heart. Isabella, Kippy and I are a threesome now, and of course there is an awful void, but we endure. Before too long, there will be a fourth to join us, as Isabella is expecting our first grandchild. She tells me that if it is a girl, she will be named Sophia. I live alone in the charming Dower House, which I believe Sophia loved more than any place we'd ever lived. The *Abbey* has been reincarnated into a stunning hotel, and people come from all over the world to see what it was like to live there when it was a true home, back before the war. I've become quite a gardener in my own right, and I know Sophia would be proud of that.

I miss her. I miss her laughter. I miss her sweet smile. I miss the way she never went to sleep without first making certain she'd told me she loved me, and the way she would waken during the night and pull the covers up around me, as though I were a child. Most of all, I miss the love we shared. Now, I'm the only one who remembers. I feel as if a part of me is missing, and the pain from that loss is just as real as if someone had taken off an arm or a leg. Sophia and I were one soul, and we both always believed we would go through time in such a manner. It's true. I know that I'll see her again, not just on the other side, which I believe *will* happen, but in another lifetime, that God has designed just for us. I don't know where it will be, but I know there will be paperwhite's, and jonquils, and of course, roses. Masses and masses of roses. Wherever that special place, we shall look at one another, and know, just as we did in 1935. It will be clear that each of us has found the one God intended for the other. I look forward to that time. I long for it. I don't know if she will be dark haired, or fair, tall or short, shy or sassy. But I'll know that it's her. And I will take her into my arms again, like it was the very first time, but her old soul eyes will give her away, just as they did the last time. And many times before, I'm certain. God chose us for one another long ago, and He will do so again. We are soul mates, and soul mates are destined to never leave their other half for any prolonged period. Therefore, I know it won't be long before I hold her in my arms again, and we both smile and say to one another "*Serendipity*."

Other Books by Mary Christian Payne

The Somerville Trilogy
Willow Grove Abbey: Book 1 of the Somerville Trilogy
St. James Road: Book 2 of the Somerville Trilogy
Serendipity: Book 3 of the Somerville Trilogy

The Claybourne Trilogy
The White Feather: Book 1 of the Claybourne Trilogy
The White Butterfly: Book 2 of the Claybourne Trilogy
White Cliffs of Dover: Book 3 of the Claybourne Trilogy

The Thornton Trilogy
No Regrets: Book 1 of The Thornton Trilogy
No Gentleman: Book 2 of the Thornton Trilogy
No Secrets: Book 3 of the Thornton Trilogy

About The Author

Mary Christian Payne was highly successful in several management positions in Fortune 500 Companies, in New York City, St. Louis, Missouri, Orlando Florida, and Tulsa, Oklahoma. Her work included Grant writing, and designing and writing Training Manuals for Executive Training Programs.

She left the corporate world, and became Director of Career Development at the Women' Resource Center at the University of Tulsa, where she designed a program that enabled hundreds of adult women to return to college and better their lives. She received the Mayor's Pinnacle Award in 1993 for this achievement. Mary left that position when the Center closed, and then opened her own Career Counseling Center. She retired in 2008.

Mary Christian Payne became a successful, best-selling author at the age of 71, with the help of her publisher, Tom Corson-Knowles. All of her life, she had wanted to write, and had received accolades for her unpublished work. She was encouraged in college, and writing was a significant part of the various jobs she held.

In 2013, she read Tom Corson-Knowles' book about publishing on Kindle. She wrote to him and he telephoned her. The rest is history. Since that time, she has published nine books, with more on the way.

Mary lost her husband in June, 2015, after 33 years of marriage. The grief process brought a lull to her writing, but she found that putting words on paper helped immensely. She is now in the process of writing her second novel since his death. She lives in Tulsa, Oklahoma, with her two beloved Maltese dogs.

One Last Thing...

If you enjoyed this book, I'd be very grateful if you'd post a short review. Your support really does make a difference and I read all the reviews personally.

Thanks again for your support!

Sign up for the newsletter to get news, updates and new release info from Mary Christian Payne: http://bit.ly/MaryChristianPayne